The Extraordinary Magic Of Everyday Life

The Extraordinary Magic of Everyday Life
ISBN-13: 978-0-578-01081-6
Lulu.com

The Extraordinary Magic

of

Everyday Life

Judy Cicero Hilbert

Judy Cicero Hilbert, Ph.D. is a retired professor and mental health clinician who focused her career on women's lives and concerns. She is particularly curious about the relationships among women of all ages and the enrichment women's friendships can offer across a lifetime. She is the author of 'The Lady Series' which includes *The Salt Shaker Lady* and *The Straight Laced Lady in the Cock-eyed Hat,* both short stories. Her newest story is a children's fairy tale, *Tate and the Lotus Pond.*

Judy is the wife of Harvey Hilbert, the mother of Samantha Cicero, Jason Cicero and Jacob Hilbert, and the grandmother of Samie, Livvy, and Tate.

These folks may be seen in some of her stories!

Enjoy!

Dedicated

To my very special grandchildren—

Samie, Livvy & Tate

And

To Eve and Deana,

extraordinary friends who helped form this trio

With all my love

Acknowledgements

To my husband, Harvey, I offer my deepest appreciation and devotion for his constant support of my creative endeavors from doll making to creative writing. His talents as a writer and his faith in my abilities enabled me to continue with this amusing effort to its completion.

My children, and granddaughter Samie have provided continual encouragement. The small ones, Livvy and Tate, remain steady as my muses.

Throughout this process the feedback and patience from the Desert Writers group members was remarkable. Our leader and guide, Kevin McIlvoy, offered confidence in my writing efforts. And finally, to my dear friends, Deana, Eve, and the others to whom I subjected my drafts of this work, I thank you.

You are the magic

Prologue: 1973

J ake felt fuzzy. Hours of touching, tugging, and washing had straightened his tightly curled fur. In spite of all the loving attention, he carried tufts of matted fur, sections of furlessness, and small craters of dirt and dust. Dixie Lou, Jake's owner, resolved to make him whole; clean, smooth, and appealing.

Dixie Lou's therapist suggested her constant attention to Jake's welfare bordered on obsession. "You know, Dixie Lou," she said, "it's time to give up that old, tattered teddy bear. Throw it away. It's a painful reminder of your past. You need to put it behind you. Move on now."

Dixie Lou shifted in her chair, cuddling Jake closer to her heart. She seemed to drift off a little, then shook herself and looked at her therapist. "There's more to Jake than you know," she said cautiously. "He's not just an old, tattered teddy bear, a childhood toy. True, I found him in a trash can, dirty and all, but that wasn't our first encounter." She cleared her throat and continued. "You see, my mama gave him to me when I was real little."

She thought for a second. "Maybe when I was born. Don't remember ever bein' without him. Then Mama died." She took a deep breath and went on without a word from her therapist. "Daddy was real mad. Wouldn't talk. Just sat around our apartment still like. Thinkin', I guess. Cryin' a lot too. So it got real quiet at our place. At night, I would just go to bed. By myself. Daddy didn't care. Oh, he fed me and all, but really just stayed to himself. All I had left was Jake. So I began talkin' to him at night. Night after night. Cried. Tried to make sense of our lives without Mama. One night, I was about to give up and be like Daddy. Just stop talkin, carin'. That night in bed, Jake poked me. He did! I about jumped out of my skin. Thought I was goin' crazy for sure. Then *he* started talkin'. Sayin' all the things I thought about. Sayin' all the things I talked to him about. Then assurin' me we would be all right. Well, after a while, I began talkin' back to him. One evening, when Daddy was just sittin' in his chair, starin' and mopin', I forgot he was there and began talkin to Jake out loud. Well that got Daddy's attention all right. He got really mad, scared me. Said he wouldn't let me go crazy like Mama, talkin' to things that weren't there. He grabbed Jake from me and told me to go to bed. I cried and begged to have Jake back but that made him madder. Finally, I fell asleep, alone and afraid. Sometime later, Daddy picked Jake up and marched out to the trashcan, where it was real dark in the back alley, and shoved Jake in. I heard him leave, looked out my window and saw what he did. The next morning when he went to work, I rescued Jake. By then he was dirty, smelly, but with me forever. Even in Nam." A long silence followed. Dixie Lou finally said, "He's all the love Mama had for us, even if she wouldn't talk to us but did talk out loud to people who weren't there. I often wished Daddy could have seen this, but he was too far gone in grief to believe in magic," Dixie Lou finished after wiping her eyes with the back of her hand. "He's my only hope to make sense out of the senseless."

With that, Dixie Lou decided she'd had enough. Enough talkin' about how hard it is to talk. Enough tryin' to relate to those who hadn't been there. Enough of this silly therapist who insisted she give up the only stable, loving friend she'd ever had. Through it all, Jake had been there. Steady, predictable, forgivin'. Couldn't say that for most people.

"I'm sorry, ma'am," she said aloud. "I just can't do this talkin' stuff anymore. You're right. I need to move along. Do something. But it will be with Jake. Thanks for your help and all." Looking into her bag, Dixie Lou softly said, "Gotta go, don't we, Jake. Let's go now." And without another word, she gently settled Jake down in his bag, slung him over her shoulder and left the Veterans' Outreach Center with a lighter step than she had experienced for a long time. "Yep Jake, it's time to move on all right. Just you and me again."

When they reached the outer door, the freezing air snapped Dixie Lou's breath away. Although she had been raised in New York, two tours in the jungles of Nam had acclimatized her toward much hotter, humid weather. "The tropics were probably better for my health but not my safety," she said to Jake as she shivered and smiled sadly. "And strangely I felt more alive there than here back in the World."

Tucking her long jacket more tightly around her slight frame, and pulling Jake closer under her arm, she pushed her way out of the building and joined the anonymous mass of New Yorkers making their way through the City to whatever self-important destination they had selected. "I say we go back, Jake, back to where we came from. Back to being alone. We can figure out what to do once we get there. What do you think?" she asked. She thought she heard a small muffled voice from inside the bag say "sure." Jake's confirmation was all Dixie Lou needed.

Dixie Lou found herself walking toward her old neighborhood. Hugging the buildings to catch a bit of warmth, she still felt the cold permeate her bones. She shivered continuously and gritted her teeth, causing her jaw to ache. As she neared the Majestic Theater, she noticed the side door ajar. This old theater had been abandoned for years but was a familiar stomping ground to Dixie Lou when she was a child. Many times, alone, she would sneak into the old movie house, with Jake in her pocket, and sit for hours watching movie after movie with other latchkey kids and old, drunken men. The kids were wise to the company of the winos, left them alone and sat up in the balcony where it was safe. The temptation to sneak into the theater was triggered by its potential warmth but cradled by its familiar memories of comfort and seclusion. In no time, Dixie Lou and Jake were inside.

"Remember this place, Jake? Don't be afraid," Dixie Lou whispered. "It's just dark. Nobody's here. We'll go up to the to balcony. Scoot down in that old, red velvety seat and catch a little nap. Then we can figure out what to do next. Have to warm up a bit first. Cold air hurts my chest. Don't worry, though, I'll be okay. Just need to warm up, ya know." With that, Dixie Lou began making her way across the back of the auditorium toward the steps to the balcony. Her legs were stiff from the cold, and she stumbled loudly.

"Who's that?" a loud, gruff voice demanded. "Halt! Who are you? "

Dixie Lou stopped abruptly. Silent, still, alert, she scanned the front of the theater to discern a clearer image of the speaker. The sound seemed to come from the first row, left-hand corner. Dixie Lou couldn't see who it was. The darkness was embracing and it took a few moments for her eyes to adjust.

"I said go way. Now! At once! Don't come closer. I'm warning you," shouted the man now visible in silhouette against the sidewall. He appeared to be rather large and bulky. His face was obscured by a full mountain-man beard that was either salt-and-pepper gray or just plain dirty. He was silent for a few seconds awaiting Dixie Lou's response.

Dixie Lou's military training was in saving lives, not taking them. As a nurse, she knew how to quietly and competently respond to soldiers who were terrified, panicky, and in severe pain. For the better part of the past two years she had worked her medical magic in operating theaters less comfortable and more dangerous than this old movie house. And with patients much less rational than this voice in the darkness. She wasn't afraid.

"Hello," she said calmly. "I'm Dixie Lou, just back in the World. What about you?" She knew the reference to 'the World' would indicate her veteran status and appeal to a fellow insider. The insider/outsider phenomenon common among Nam vets was widespread and deeply felt. She hoped it would serve her well now.

After a short pause, the man's voice replied in a respectful tone, "Welcome home." Another pause and then he continued. "Just don't come close. We'll talk from here."

"Okay. When'd ya get back?"

"'Bout a month ago. Name's Joe. My brother Sam's here too."

With that brief introduction, a more gentle voice stated, "Welcome home, Dixie Lou. Don't mind Joe. He's always gruff. Tries to stay angry. Keeps people afraid and away. Thinks we have each other, can live here, and that's enough. Crazy, huh?"

"Yeah," chuckled Dixie Lou. "Well, if you think that's weird, my best and only buddy is my stuffed teddy bear, Jake. What's more, he can talk." She waited for their reaction to her announcement fairly certain Jake would be accepted as fact without proof. Most veterans had seen enough craziness in meaningless combat that a talking teddy bear should be oddly amusing.

"Well," said Joe, "you can come down here a little closer where we can see you." Without skipping a beat he added, "Bring the bear."

Dixie Lou was no fool. While she yearned for the company of other veterans, she knew not all soldiers were 'friendlies'. As a woman and an officer, Dixie Lou was well aware of those gung-ho guys who needed to puff out their chests, lower their voices, and thunder their orders in a show of their machismo. She knew she needed to be cautious with two strange men. More than her gender, though, her health worried her as she experienced trouble catching her breath, especially when anxious or stressed. "Be there in a moment," she stated, and practiced the deep breathing exercises she had been taught at the VA. In a short time, her chest seemed to open, and a rush of stale air entered her lungs. She felt better and more secure, ready to make her way down towards the front of the theater.

When Dixie Lou and Jake were halfway toward the front row, Joe yelled, "Far enough. Sit there. We can talk from here." Dixie Lou smiled at the familiar manner of speaking common among men used to giving orders. "Yes sir," she offered, slipping into soldier speak.

"Now," continued Joe. "Tell us who you are and what you want."

Sam added, "And a little more about Jake."

"Well," Dixie Lou began, settling herself and Jake into an aisle seat, her back to the side wall. "Been in Nam last two years as an Army nurse. Worked in field hospitals, medevac units. Planned to make a career of it but developed breathin' problems so I had to leave. Thought I'd come home, live with my Daddy until I figured out what to do, but that didn't work out. Been goin' for help at the Vet Center, but that didn't work either. Gotta figure it out for myself. What about you guys?"

"My brother and me served together as Spec 4s up in the Highlands. Mostly recon. Did our tour and wanted out as fast as we could. Feel lucky to be here. Just don't fit in much anywhere. Wives left us. No kids. Parents gone so we're traveling a bit, like you, to find a place to settle. This old theater is temporary for us. Good for the cold weather and being alone. Until now," he chuckled.

"We figure you for Captain or Major in Nam," Joe added.

Dixie Lou let his speculation pass. "So," she went on, "I think this place is big enough for all of us. Just want to rest a spell myself. Won't bother you. We kinda like it up in the balcony and plan to sleep a bit until the day warms up. Okay with you?"

"Not until we see that Bear," grumbled Joe. "And be real slow removing him from your bag. We're watching you."

Dixie Lou was immediately relieved. Her experience with Jake taught her that others' reaction to Jake, most notably the pronoun selected to refer to him, was telling. Calling Jake *him* was a really good sign. "We made it okay," she whispered to Jake as she removed him from his traveling bag. "Now go slow and easy with them. They're just heart-wounded men and can use the comfort and healin' you can offer. Let them touch you, cuddle a bit if needed, and silently reminisce about better times. Work your magic on them, okay?" Jake wiggled with excitement and anticipation. With unconditional warmth and compassion, he welcomed all who acknowledged him.

Dixie Lou passed Jake down to the brothers. Sam quickly looked at Jake, held him to his chest for a few moments and then handed him to Joe. Joe, too, relaxed, and suddenly laughed out loud. "Damn bear," he said. "Looks just like the one Gram gave us as kids, don't he, Sam. Old and tattered. But wise-looking," he concluded. "Damn bear," he said one more time as he handed Jake back to Dixie Lou. "Guess you both can stay."

Joe nodded and Sam offered Dixie Lou a small blanket he had in his backpack. Gratefully, Dixie Lou accepted the offering and moved back toward the rear of the theater. "If you want to talk more, come on down sometime," Sam suggested. "Rest well."

They all settled into their respective sections of the theater. A peculiar quartet of wizened soldiers in their late twenties and a talking teddy bear just trying to fit in.

Chapter One: 2003

"Geez Kate, slow down!" Sunny cautioned gently. "You're always in such a hurry. We'll get our spot. It's not quite lunch time, and no one new eats here anyways," Sunny added as Kate sped into the diner's parking lot, her old Woodie station wagon squeaking and sputtering just begging for a tune-up. They were headed for their favorite restaurant, a local hangout of sorts for the gray-haired set. The diner offered free refills of coffee, morning papers left on tables, and waitresses who knew when to intercede and when to leave customers alone.

Kate and Sunny, friends for over thirty years, lunched weekly at the diner. They were the first two customers to eat at the counter when the place opened in Rio Rojo, New Mexico, a small, quaint town near the Mexican border.

"Well, if you'd been ready on time, we wouldn't have to make it up," Kate complained as she swiftly parked the car and threw open her door. "You know I can't stand being late!"

Recently Kate was more self centered and impatient than usual. "Who's waiting for us?" Sunny softly countered, pulling herself together, used to her old friend's idiosyncrasies. "No one," she continued. "What difference does it make anyways?"

"It makes a difference to me," Kate said as she quickly jumped out of her car and started toward the diner's entrance. Forgetting about Sunny's difficulty with hearing, she continued speaking over her shoulder. "Says something about me, about being organized, about managing time, about…."

"Oh please," Sunny scoffed gently, unaware of Kate's exact words but familiar with her general complaints. "You always make such a personal big deal out of everything. People hardly pay attention to two old ladies like us, so let's not create a fuss," she said as she struggled to catch up with Kate.

Out of the corner of her eye, Sunny noticed their reflections in the restaurant window—Kate, tall and lean, straight back, long, white hair tied up tightly in a bun. Make-up perfect and appropriate. Clothes slightly tailored, laundered. She walked quickly, with small, determined steps.

Sunny was petite, slightly paunchy around her middle and bent over a bit, using her walking stick these days for balance. Her once red hair was pinkish now, laced with white and blond sections, the result of natural aging and years of hair dye. Her favorite long cotton skirt was well washed and soft to the touch. It hung crooked, however, listing to the left. Her embroidered Mexican blouse was worn but colorful. Both women were in their early sixties and were best friends.

As they entered the restaurant, Kate whispered to Sunny, "Your skirt is hitched up a bit on one side. Better go fix it."

"Thanks, but we're just going to sit down now so it won't be noticed anyways," Sunny replied. Her arthritis was acting up, and she simply wanted to sit down.

Sunny and Kate took their usual seats at the counter and looked around for Marge, their first and favorite waitress. Marge was busy at the other end bussing the remains from four truckers who ate well and left good tips. Marge had grown with the diner both in service and stature. Fifty-five years old now and 185 pounds, she served her customers with flair and warmth and herself with her daily favorite meal of cube steak with mushrooms and brown gravy, mashed potatoes with loads of butter and sour cream, cooked vegetables smothered in cheese sauce, a cloverleaf roll or two, and, of course, Dutch apple pie à la mode.

Sunny looked around. The breakfast regulars were still there eating their doughnuts and sipping coffee. One table with six elderly men was raucous as usual. In fact, one old guy looked at Sunny and winked. She felt her face flush. A warm memory flashed through her mind of an evening of two-stepping and kissing long ago.

By unspoken affirmation, this 'men's table' drew a diverse group of white-haired elders who argued amiably about everything from the stock market to the advent of Viagra. This table had been unofficially reserved over the years for the men in town who needed and welcomed the company of their peers. Occasionally the group was comprised of retired professionals—lawyers still arguing classic cases, professors capturing an audience in order to pontificate, CPAs discussing IRAs and 401Ks. Today it was made up of ordinary guys, chatting about baseball, their grandkids, or their deceased wives. Frequently the men's group was mixed racially, with one old black guy chatting it up with a couple of Hispanics and a few Anglos. The charm of this mixed group was that at one time this restaurant was open only to a racially homogenous crowd. Blacks, whites, and Hispanics had their place, and it wasn't with one another. Now they lounged together sharing equally and comfortably in one another's world. By far, the conversational meanderings of this group were the most stimulating of the diner's crowd.

"My God, Sunny, look at the *really* old lady over there," Kate said, nodding toward the end of the counter. Her nose seemed to turn up as she spoke. "Looks dirty. Skin's almost gray. Smelly too, *I bet*. And that awful bag she has on her lap. It's overflowing. You suppose there's bugs and stuff in there? She probly sleeps on the ground and things crawl in at night. Shouldn't be allowed to eat here. Nope. It's a *health* hazard. Just give her some leftover 'to go' food and send her on her way."

"Kate, hush up, she'll hear you," Sunny whispered as she bent over toward Kate.

"I don't care," Kate grumbled. "She should have more pride in herself than to sit at a counter, looking dirty like that, and expect to be served with people like us. Why doesn't she just go to the soup kitchen, where her friends might be? They're used to each other."

With that, the old lady extracted a tattered teddy bear from her bag. "Didcha hear that?" she said in a quivering voice. "That uppity one thinks we don't deserve to be in public. Wants to keep us apart, away from her and her friend." She paused and leaned even closer to her bear. "What?" she said. "Think we should move? Okay." Picking up her bag and teddy bear in shaky hands, she moved down and sat right next to Kate.

"Oh my *God*," Kate whispered as she inched closer toward Sunny.

"Hi. I'm Dixie Lou. Meet my best friend, Jake," the bag lady sputtered, holding out her bear. Kate jumped back, almost toppling off her chair. Sunny giggled at Kate's reaction but quickly covered this with a fake cough.

Dixie Lou coughed as well, and her voice became more breathy. She quickly took a small sip of Kate's water. "Thanks," she said, addressing Kate. "We've been travelin' a while, Jake and me, and we saw you nice ladies and decided to say hey." Looking at Jake, she instructed, "Say hello."

Kate gasped and Sunny quickly replied before Kate could embarrass her further with some kind of defensive sarcasm. "Hi," she said, then added, "to both of you. Where you from?"

Without skipping a beat, Dixie Lou turned to her bear as if he could reply. "He said we're from back East," she said. "He's a li'l pushy," Dixie Lou added quickly, "so I'll talk for him. He's been with me for forty-five years at least. Rescued him from a trashcan, I did. In Brooklyn, lonely and scared. Kinda dirty too. So was I— scared that is. Lived with my daddy there but was alone a lot 'cause he went out every day to find work. Was so glad to have a new friend. And we got along so well, been together a long time. No matter what he's always there for me. Helps me get by for sure."

Rolling her eyes, Kate scoffed, "*Helps* you? How in the world could he *help* you? He's just an old, stuffed teddy bear. A kid's toy. Why, it's even silly to think of him as a *he* rather than the trashy toy *it* is."

Against her better judgment, however, Kate felt drawn to this strange woman, confused by Dixie Lou's simple openness and friendliness. And by her obvious disregard for their different stations in life. This appalled Kate. Struggling to remain polite yet detached, Kate took a deep breath, pursed her lips, and impatiently waited for the conversation to end.

Kate's question, however, was not dismissed by Dixie Lou but rather taken quite seriously as she answered, "Jake helps me by listenin'. He gives advice, even scolds me sometimes. Talks kind to me mostly. Tells me to be honest, remember not everyone is as lucky as us. Always willin' to do whatever I want without complaint. Travels contentedly in his bag. Never had a better friend, have you?"

Kate looked at Sunny and smiled. "Everyone should be so lucky," she said.

Marge wiped up the counter and edged closer, within earshot, to this strange threesome. The counter was filled with customers who also took notice of Dixie Lou and her unusual appearance. Dixie Lou was dressed in a clean but oversized sweater with holes on the elbows. Underneath this sweater peeked a man's dress shirt, one tip of the collar sticking up into her chin. Her loose-fitting, black sweat pants sagged at the knees. She wore heavy sport socks and blue Keds. She wrapped a brightly colored scarf around her head, held in place by an artificial, large red rose. Her pale face was lined and full of worry. It was difficult to determine her age and actual size. At first glance she appeared fragile.

Marge nodded at Dixie Lou, inviting her presence without comment. While uncommon to have a bag lady at her counter, Marge made no judgments on appearance. Over the years she worked here, she could tell the good people from the bad, heard many tales, and became adept at discerning truth from fiction. To several others at the counter, and certainly to Kate, Marge's unquestioning acceptance of Dixie Lou's story, and of this strange bear, bordered on crazy. Actually, to them, *Dixie Lou* was pushing the edges of sanity.

And Dixie Lou liked it this way. Her need to connect with people was predicated solely on her need to survive. Whatever it takes, she thought, to get a bite to eat. Even a little company is okay, she resolved, and acting crazy kept most people at arm's length. Jake's all I really need, she thought uneasily as she watched Sunny and Kate's comfortable companionship with one another.

Kate glanced at Marge and seemed unsettled. Dixie Lou grinned, the teddy bear on a stool beside her. Sunny, excited, simply ordered lunch——for four.

Chapter Two

With the peculiar entrance of Dixie Lou into their world, Kate and Sunny's long friendship suddenly took a sharp turn toward a tension unfamiliar to them. Typically they moved along with their established understandings and disagreements, secure in the knowledge that whatever occurred would enrich them both. In their younger days, these friends struggled with petty competitions and jealousies, but over time smoothed out such inconsequential difficulties and cemented their differences with compassion and love. This time, however, an invisible barrier arose between them.

The following day, up earlier than usual, Kate took a quick shower, fixed her hair and make-up, and sat at her antique kitchen table in her tiny breakfast nook, struggling with her thoughts. A creature of habit, Kate needed the routine of the ordinary to maintain her inner sense of calm. Change worried her, foretelling the unknown, which had been a threatening circumstance in Kate's history.

"Well," she muttered to herself, taking a sip of coffee and sitting up even straighter in her hard-backed chair. "I'm a good woman, always have been. I like to help out the poor and crippled. After all, I save up money to donate each Christmas to those needy children. Even helped at the soup kitchen once until the smell got to me. Seems like we've done our duty buying that Dixie Lou lunch yesterday. Should be enough, I think. Now she's probly gonna latch on to us like a Velcro leech, and then what do we do?"

With her anxiety mounting and anger bubbling over her good sense, Kate called Sunny.

Sunny liked to 'lie in' and enjoy her early morning dreamy musings undisturbed. She called this her 'float time'. Usually she would arise early, make a cup of peach tea, poke her head outside to check the stars, feed Madame Luna, her African Gray parrot, and then return to her bed with her dog, Chloe.

Madame Luna was a middle-aged bird by now, having joined Sunny's family when she was a baby, close to forty years ago. She spent her baby years in Sunny's Tea Shop, learning to speak and interact with people through the customers who visited and chatted with her. A demanding bird, Madame Luna was intelligent and loyal, affectionate with Sunny and Sunny's close friends. With luck and continued good care, she could live another twenty years or so.

On the other hand, Chloe's age was unknown, but most of Sunny's friends *believed* Chloe had lived with Sunny since Sunny was a small child. She just had that manner about her——forever present. In fact, this Chloe was the great-great granddaughter of the original

Chloe, and carried the characteristic calm common to her hybrid breeding. Both she and Sunny were annoyed when the phone rang and interrupted their cozy reverie.

"Yes Kate," Sunny answered, checking caller ID before picking up her phone—a small concession to her granddaughter, who worried needlessly about Sunny's willingness to talk to anyone about anything.

"Are you all right?"

"Course I'm okay," Kate snapped. "Have to tell you I'm just upset with you. I can't understand why you invited that dirty old bag lady we met yesterday over for brunch today. Are you going senile on me? Why, she'll probly steal from us. Or pretend to choke on food so she can sue us. What if she's casing the place so her friends can break in later and take stuff from us? You know, they need stuff to put in their bags from time to time. Besides, what kind of a person is named Dixie Lou and is from New York? Something is really fishy here. Oh Sunny, what have you gotten us into now? Let's just go out looking for her, give her some money, and cancel the brunch," she pleaded. "Tell her we have to go volunteer at the thrift shop or something. Suggest she try eating at the women's shelter."

As Kate ranted on, her hands shook and her breath became shortened. She felt her heart beating hard inside her thin chest. This level of felt anger was uncommon to her. While Kate was quite comfortable appearing aloof and standoffish, she was not used to experiencing such intense rage. Over the years, she had learned to temper her feelings, and she worked hard toward covering them with a false, calm demeanor. What's coming over her? Kate wondered. A little late in life for me to become all touchy-feely, she thought sardonically.

Sunny, patience to match her tolerance, let Kate rant on. She knew her friend would eventually wind down and take a breath. That was the moment she awaited.

"Kate, slow down," Sunny said quickly. "Take another breath," she directed as she too breathed deeply. "Being upset isn't good for you," she cautioned, aware of her best friend's propensity for overreacting and making herself more upset. "You know I'd never do anything to hurt you. If you really don't want to have brunch with Dixie Lou, just stay home. I'll handle it alone and make your apologies." Sunny, knowing such a position would challenge her friend's basically good character, smiled at Chloe and winked. Sunny had no reservations about making new friends or helping others out. And she knew Kate knew this.

"Darn it Sunny, all right. I'll be there. But please, at least don't use your good china. And put away your silver tea service. Don't tempt fate. And be sure to call your granddaughter and tell her what we are doing. That way someone will know enough to check on us after brunch," she huffed, "to see if we're still breathing."

Sunny smiled again, and with warm affection assured Kate they were doing a good thing this one time. If truth be known, however, Sunny suspected Dixie Lou—-and Jake—might make their twosome a permanent foursome. And what fun that could be!

Deciding that a return to sleep was out of the question, Sunny got up, put on her sneakers and a hoodie, grabbed her walking stick, and headed toward the door. She slept in an old t-shirt and sweat pants, so dressing was not an issue. Chloe, ever present but reluctant to exercise, waited for her at the door with her tail between her legs. Over the years, Sunny's stamina outlasted her dog's, but without fail Chloe's devotion won out over her fatigue. Together they started out towards the 24-hour corner store, walking with confidence along the darkened dirt road that cut through the high desert surrounding her home. She was familiar with this path as she and Chloe had hiked it for years. Putting a hand in her pocket, she found the miniature finger light her granddaughter had given her for her birthday, smiled, and put it on. Its neon blue, ultra-bright LED flashed as she walked, creating an eerie sight for the few early morning passersby on the adjacent highway.

Suddenly, Chloe stopped. "Let's go, Chloe," Sunny urged. "It's chilly out here and we have lots to do today. We have to move along." Chloe refused, an uncommon reaction. Sunny stopped still.

The fur on Chloe's neck rose as she made a deep rumbling sound in her throat. A large but gentle dog by nature, she could appear threatening given her husky size and deep bark. She had never hurt anyone, even Sunny's grandchildren when they were toddlers and climbed on her back and pulled on her ears. As Sunny's long-time companion, however, she was duty bound to protect her master at all costs and for once, she sensed danger and stood ready.

"Shh, Chloe" Sunny whispered, patting Chloe on top of her head. "Just an old coyote or something looking for breakfast."

Again Chloe refused. In fact, she moved in front of Sunny and struck an attack position.

Chapter Three

A fter Dixie Lou left her new friends, Kate and Sunny, at the diner, she was far too excited to settle down quietly in the park and read. She had picked up the paper at the diner, planning to relax in the sun and catch up on the news. Instead, she wandered around aimlessly most of the day until her need to connect with kindred souls surfaced again. She decided to visit the small group of homeless men who lived under the Main Street Bridge. These vets, some without teeth and most without hair, drifted by day through town looking for company and coffee. By early evening they reconvened under the bridge to share a smoke, discuss the day, and settle in for a restless sleep. Dixie Lou was friends with the four regulars; Jim, Bud, Joe, and Sam.

"Hey Dixie Lou," the men said in unison when they spotted her.

"Have a seat," Bud offered quickly as he moved over on his blanket, rearranging his meager possessions to make room for her.

"Come join us a while here and have a sip. We got free coffee from the truck stop when Bud bought smokes," offered Sam.

"Trying to quit, he says," chided Jim. "At least we all get the benefit of the coffee along with his second-hand smoke," he joked affectionately.

"Hey fellas," Dixie Lou said, then eagerly greeted each warmly by name. "Can't stay long but wanted to chat a little. How's your day been?" she added quickly and somewhat impatiently. Uncharacteristically, she continued speaking without waiting for their replies. "Mine's been very excitin'. Met two great ladies, Kate and Sunny, and I liked them. Jake liked them too. Fixin' to go to Sunny's for brunch tomorra, can you believe it?" she asked. Her excitement was obvious. Her cheeks were flushed, and her voice was steady and strong.

Accustomed to Dixie Lou listening to them rather than talking about herself, their combined guardedness barricaded any joy they might have felt for this good lady. Each in his own way was suspicious of Dixie Lou's judgment at this moment and wary of her need to visit with two strange women.

"You don't have to go to a stranger's house to eat," Jim quickly countered. "If you need money, I got some." Jim's experiences in Nam cemented his natural reluctance to speak freely or easily. He had sustained a serious leg wound and was medically discharged contrary to his wishes.

"Me too," said Bud, always willing to share his meager earnings. He worked as a day laborer occasionally doing yard work and odd jobs for the wealthy people who lived out of town. A van from the Rescue Mission House would pick up any who wanted work at 8:00 each morning and deliver them to designated job sites. Often Bud worked these odd jobs more as a diversion than out of monetary need, as he enjoyed keeping active. "I don't need much, and I always have some left over each month. Just sitting around doing nothing, so you might as well use it."

Brothers Joe and Sam offered to hang out near the brunch site to stand guard if Dixie Lou was determined to go. "We'll surveil for you," they said, excited in fact by the prospect of doing something useful for her.

Not drinkers, these men received disability monies that were deposited monthly in some far-off bank accessible by ATMs across the country. They managed to travel at will, disconnected from family and old friends but united with others like themselves. They asked little from each other and nothing from the townspeople. Dixie Lou was one of a few women they trusted. She listened without criticism, flirted without expectation, and smiled without condescension.

"Thanks but no thanks, guys. Jake and I can take care of ourselves. We'll be okay. Tell ya'all about it later," Dixie Lou commented happily and waved good-bye. "Just wanted to keep ya'll posted. Going to the women's shelter tonight so we have to move on now. We'll look for you tomorrow. Thanks for the coffee. Take care of yourselves now, ya hear," she added, ever the nurse in the field.

"You too," said Bud with a warm smile.

Moseying on, Dixie Lou found herself huddled with a few women friends around a trash-barrel fire behind the homeless women's shelter. While many women scrambled each night to secure a cot in the shelter, this group chose to remain outside, near enough to get help if they needed it, yet liberated from the rules of worship and lights out endemic to the shelter. Wrapped in hand-knit shawls donated to the shelter's recycle shop, they looked like old sorority sisters in their uniform sweaters planning the next pledge event. In fact, not just anyone was invited into this small circle of warmth. Only women who were street-wise, older, and loners were welcomed. No hangers-on were encouraged. No young runaways, none who were sickly or addicts. Their need to be independent was strangely embraced by their nighttime need to be joined in this peculiar circle of girlfriends. They looked out for each other but at a distance and at night, for the most part. Dixie Lou was a charter member of this group as was Jake.

"Well, hey Sista" greeted one heavyset black woman. Dixie Lou imagined that a diet of Cheetos, honey buns, and Dr Peppers inflated her large belly that swayed from side to side as she meandered over. She kept it partially hidden by a loose-fitting muumuu. "Haven't seen ya for a while. Been okay?" she asked.

"Sure" Dixie Lou replied. "You?"

"Sure 'nuff," she answered. "Sugar's a might off, that's all. Gets tired more often but I'm okay." With that the circle opened and Dixie Lou assumed her customary place. The desert air was cool, and the shawls and fire just right to take the chill away. The group was quietly settling in for the night giving Dixie Lou tacit permission to privately reflect on her day's happenings. She noticed that after a few turns and scratches, Jake settled down as well, deep within his warm bag.

My, thought Dixie Lou, brunch, hmmm. Not unfamiliar with social niceties, it had been a long time since she was invited to a brunch in someone's home. What to take? A little short on cash, she decided she could pick wildflowers that abutted the highway and tie a ribbon she used for her hair around them, making a lovely gift. The wild Mexican hats and purple verbenas were especially colorful at this time. Queen Anne's lace would fill in nicely.

Now, what to wear? Cleaning herself up a bit would not be a problem in the morning as she could slip into the shelter, listen to a quick sermon, shower, eat a light breakfast, and be off with the overnight residents who were required to leave for the day *in search of work.* Dressing was the bigger problem. She had clean clothes in her bag, but they were wrinkled and obviously well worn. That would not do. Yet using her limited funds to purchase new clothes was unreasonable between checks at this time of the month. She tended to conserve in case of a real emergency, like needing a motel room on occasion if she became ill. Lately she was fatigued more often and felt achy in the mornings. She noticed she bruised more easily, her skin like parchment. And she was becoming shakier.

While the shelter's recycle shop was an option, she wanted to select and purchase her outfit rather than accepting the free handouts from the shelter staff. Free only in terms of cash——costly in terms of religious instruction. No, she thought, the Goodwill down the road had a nice variety of clean and stylish clothes at reasonable prices.

Within a few hours Dixie Lou was transformed into a respectable yet aging Southwestern hippie, clothed in a long, flowered skirt, an embroidered blouse, socks and huaraches. She splurged and bought a shiny hair clip justifying this expense against the free meal she would have that day. Her gray hair was short but thin, with wispy ends bursting free from her hair clips. She never looked quite all together but this outfit suited her best efforts. Her hand knit shawl completed her look. "Not bad for a Southern lady from Brooklyn," she chuckled. "And a homeless one at that!" she said to Jake. "Now, let's get you ready," she continued, and she began the reminiscent grooming of his almost absent fur as she often did over the years when worried, stressed, or simply aware of their life of intimate solitude. When satisfied with Jake's appearance, she announced that they were both ready for brunch and quickly headed toward the diner where she was to meet Kate for a ride to Sunny's.

Chapter Four

Kate had been a member of the Joshua Tree Old Christian Church since her early thirties when she married Charles and moved to the Southwest. Not a far move in miles but in attitude and lifestyle, light-years away. Her upbringing, as she now called it, was immediately rewritten when she met Charles. He believed she came from a well educated, sophisticated family who tragically died in a car accident while Kate was away at college. A graduate of a two-year teacher's college in the Midwest, Kate told people she accepted a teaching position in this rural, one room schoolhouse by choice to quietly and privately mourn her family in the warm, but aloof cocoon of small-town living. A slight stretch of the truth as Kate's parents were just drinking their way to a far-off but miserable demise.

Charles, not particularly bright but handsome, was an over-the-road trucker in search of a spread to settle down on. His travels included the Southwest where land was available and inexpensive, and people were friendly but kept their distance. The beauty of the land, the temperate climate, and the pioneer spirit were extremely appealing. He met Kate at the Twisted River Truck Stop where she ate her evening meal alone as she pretended to be traveling through town. He was immediately struck by her intelligence and obvious need for male companionship. She recognized he was her only hope of escaping a dismal, single life, fantasizing about her high school senior boys as she aged and despaired. They quickly married so that they could travel respectably across the country together and after a week of sight seeing and aimless driving settled in Rio Rojo. The town was near Charles' trucking headquarters, yet isolated enough to offer some anonymity that both Charles and Kate felt it could become home. Immediately they joined the Old Josh church. They appeared happy and compatible for many years until Charles left for a trucking run one summer day and simply never returned. At that moment Kate's heart snapped shut. Her growing belief that she could find a safe, predictable and happy relationship was shattered.

When townspeople asked about Charles, Kate claimed he was called home, whatever that meant, and insisted they would be together at another time. Turning her porch light on each evening, her life was spent secretly watching and waiting for that moment. Her best friend, Sunny, never questioned her behavior. Sunny's experience told her that sometimes people do just inexplicably disappear.

Kate spent ten minutes searching in her closet for something to wear. Dressing deliberately to match the occasion, she finally donned her best white cotton summer dress, edged in hand-made lace. She bought it at the Mercado in Mexico when she and Charles crossed over to shop one day, but had not worn it in many years. Too much like a wedding dress, she thought, and ached a little when she put it on. Taking a deep breath, pulling her shoulders back, she resolved to wear it with ease and grace. My nice turquoise squash-blossom necklace and wide bracelet to match will work nicely, she thought. As a tall, broad-shouldered woman, she could wear this heavy Navajo jewelry well. A pair of silver earrings, casual Birkenstock sandals, center braid of white hair down her back, and she was ready. What would this day bring?

When Kate drove into the parking lot at the restaurant, she didn't recognize Dixie Lou standing alongside the building. Feeling justified for her general annoyance with this situation, she fought to remain calm and patient. Her fingers began tapping on her steering wheel. Before she could turn off the engine, however, Dixie Lou was looking in the side window with a large smile on her face.

"Holy cow, Dixie Lou, you startled me. Don't sneak up on people like that. Could get you in a lot of trouble!" Kate remarked. Dixie Lou smiled again at the irony of this observation and how little Kate knew.

The long walk from the shelter to the restaurant in the morning desert air left Dixie Lou feeling chilled but invigorated. She was a little short of breath, but who wouldn't be after that walk?

Swinging her new-used small shoulder bag onto the front seat, she got in quickly.

"Wouldja mind turnin the heater on a bit?" she asked, trembling.

"For heaven's sake, Dixie Lou, gas is high enough without using it up on heat. Just sit still a while and you'll warm up. Here, grab that old blanket in the back seat. Old, but clean," she wisecracked.

Dixie Lou, unaffected by this mild scolding, happily complied. She put her bag on her lap under the blanket so Jake could also warm up.

With a captive audience, Kate decided a little impolite poking into Dixie Lou's background was in order. No one would know, she thought. Sunny would never do such a thing, but Kate struggled with this odd woman who had so permeated their friendship in such a short time. She hoped to trip her up, especially about her delusional teddy bear. Then she could convince Sunny to give up their relationship with this crazy old bag lady.

"So" she began "staying in town long?"

"Hard to say. Depends on Jake".

Aha, her opening! "Uh, Jake. Exactly what *is* Jake, do you think? Kinda your imaginary friend, I guess. Sorta easy to believe in this stuff I suppose if you have no real friends." Then quickly recognizing her obvious snottiness, she covered with "I mean, traveling around so much."

Growing up with alcoholic parents, Kate learned how *not* to behave. Her need to present a normal, even perfect picture of herself to the world was sharply honed after all these years. She had an edge about her, however, and slipped into sarcasm when she was socially uncomfortable. This occurred most often when meeting someone like Dixie Lou who was so difficult to immediately pigeonhole as a particular personality type.

The dimple in Dixie Lou's cheek flickered for a second. Over the years she sorted people into a few general categories given their response to Jake. Those who ignored him, sort of like the elephant in the living room. Those who embraced him, like Sunny. And those who tenaciously resisted him. Like Kate. People like Kate posed the greatest challenge.

Again that enigmatic smile, Kate thought. Didn't this woman ever get rattled? Before she could answer, Kate continued, "I mean, it's against God's nature, you know. To try and fool people that your teddy bear can talk. Almost like a devil was inside you. Some folks might even think that—that you are possessed or crazy."

With that, there seemed to be a slight movement under the blanket on Dixie Lou's lap. Kate pretended not to notice it. Her heart was racing, however, as she considered she was driving in a car with a woman she had just called crazy and who had some strange twitches going on in her lap.

Oh geez, now what have I done? she thought. She'll probly go berserk and attack me. To Dixie Lou Kate said, "Just kidding of course, but talking to a teddy bear is a little strange, don't you think?"

Dixie Lou simply answered "No, not at all."

Sighing deeply, Kate changed the subject to small talk and drove on, in a hurry to get to Sunny's and the familiar comfort of her friend's presence.

Chapter Five

W hen Kate and Dixie Lou drove up to Sunny's small adobe home right on time for brunch, Chloe did not run out to greet them.

"Strange," Kate muttered, somewhat miffed. "Chloe must be inside and hasn't heard us. Probly going deaf like Sunny." She parked the Woodie and stepped out quickly. Dixie Lou, with muffled groans, moved more slowly and painfully, her bag slung over her shoulder.

"That's funny, no smoke from the fireplace," Kate remarked as she increased her strides toward the house.

As usual, Sunny's door was unlocked and Kate immediately entered calling out her friend's name. Madame Luna chirped, "Adios, going shopping. Adios, going shopping."

"Quiet, Madame Luna," Kate snapped. "Now, where's Sunny? Table's not set. Don't smell coffee either. Nothing's baking. Don't even see any groceries out for brunch. I know Sunny was going to the store this morning early. Something's wrong here, Dixie

Lou. Very wrong! You check outside, I'll search the house," she ordered.

Dixie Lou was calm, methodical in her walk around Sunny's yard, listening and looking for any sign of life. She could hear Kate anxiously and impatiently calling for Sunny throughout the house.

After a short while, Kate met Dixie Lou outside. "Let's walk down the road a bit and see if we can find her," Kate suggested, her irritation turning to concern. Surviving in a crisis-ridden home as a child, Kate was quite adept at taking charge and taking action but without thought.

"No," said Dixie Lou, aware that it might be necessary to have a vehicle available. "Let's take the Woodie."

Annoyed with Dixie Lou's impertinence, Kate then quickly instructed her to get in the car, jumped in herself and spun her wheels tearing out of the driveway. She began to speed down Sunny's dirt road toward the nearest convenience store.

Dixie Lou gripped the suicide handle on the car's ceiling and cradled Jake tightly in her lap. Her heart beat rapidly, and she felt light-headed. Not so much afraid of Sunny's situation at the moment, Dixie Lou was more anxious about Kate's driving. Dixie Lou was fully confident that she could handle Sunny's circumstance, as her experiences with emergency nursing equipped her to react with knowledge and quiet calm. It was the unpredictable reactions of Kate that worried her.

When they rounded the first bend, they saw groceries all over the road and a blinking neon blue light lying along the side. Kate slammed on the brakes, skidded to a stop and bolted out of the car. Jake tumbled out of Dixie Lou's lap and fell to the floor with a small *oomph*.

"That's Sunny's light," Kate exclaimed. "Her granddaughter gave it to her. And look, Chloe's collar. What's happened to them? Oh, where are they?" Kate chocked back a sob, uncharacteristic and unexpected, as she picked up the light and collar.

Dixie Lou gently placed a hand on Kate's shoulder and led her back to the car. "Why dontcha get in," she said. "I'll drive, you look for them". We'll go slow. We'll find them. They'll be all right." Dixie Lou's quiet assurance calmed Kate for the moment and she complied without complaint.

When Dixie Lou sat down behind the steering wheel, she remembered she had never driven a car in her life. Growing up in Brooklyn, leaving home to become an Army nurse, then traveling by her wits for years, she simply had not needed to learn. Well, she thought, this is as good a time as any, and stepped on the accelerator. The engine raced, but the car did not move.

"Put it in gear," Kate barked. Dixie Lou did, and with a few bounces and jolts, they inched slowly along.

In a few moments Kate yelled, "Stop. Over there, by that big mesquite bush. I see something on the ground." With the car still rolling, Kate opened the door and began to get out. Inadvertently she kicked Jake out, and he rolled toward the mesquite.

Dixie Lou reached over and grabbed Kate's arm. "Stay put," she said softly. "And be still. Need to think this through. Could all be in danger."

Suddenly Kate realized that Sunny could be the victim of a horrible attack rather than a little old lady that may have tripped and fallen. She sucked in her breath and held it, trying to calm her racing heart.

While Kate and Dixie Lou sat for a moment to consider their next move, Jake rolled down a small slope and bumped up against Chloe, who was slumped by the large bush. The big dog was so still she could be mistaken for a fallen log. Jake's small paw seemed to swat Chloe, and his tiny bear claws scratched a delicate spot on Chloe's nose. Chloe, startled, awoke and shook her head, knocking Jake over. "Hey," Jake said as he tumbled for a few feet, and then landed in the soft sand of an arroyo. Chloe, alert now, quickly stood on guard, eyes moving, scanning the area. Her nose sniffed and twitched, her ears erect in search of sounds. Every muscle quivered at attention. She spotted Jake, approached him cautiously, sniffing him quickly but thoroughly. Chloe then gently picked him up in her huge mouth and carried him by the scruff of his neck. They took off in the direction Chloe's nose led them, with Jake acting much like a secondary rudder. Occasionally he shifted his weight and headed Chloe right toward Sunny as if sensing her essence.

The sun was fiercely warming the day. Without water and the proper clothing, Kate and Dixie Lou could not search long on foot in the desert for their friend. Kate might think she could do it, but

Dixie Lou, experienced in moving through the outdoors safely and wisely, and cognizant of the mounting tightness in her chest, knew they needed help in a hurry. But who? And how? After a few quiet moments Dixie Lou said, "Kate, I've some friends that can help. Good at trackin'. Strong, dedicated, care about others. We need to get them right away. You drive, I'll tell ya where to go." Kate hesitated but followed Dixie Lou's directions without argument. The thought of losing Sunny was overwhelming.

In no time, Kate and Dixie Lou were at the Main Street Bridge and picked up four scruffy-looking men along with their blankets, water, and flashlights. They quickly returned to the desert road. With practiced ease and minimal conversation, the men morphed into a four-man search and rescue team with a designated point man and a plan. They instructed Kate and Dixie Lou to slowly ride along the road with their doors locked but on the lookout for other traffic and helpers. Then they headed into the desert in search of one small lady and her very large dog.

Within an hour, the team had covered a radius of two miles. Jackrabbits, horny toads, and nesting birds startled as they approached. They discovered Chloe's distinctive tracks from her Keds in the sand and now on her trail, they covered ground easily. When they spotted Chloe, their hearts quickened, their senses sharpened. Chloe lay down with her large paw over a slight form and a funny teddy bear at her side.

They had found Sunny.

A makeshift gurney was constructed from the blankets the men had. The team gently positioned Sunny on it, offered her water, and then carried her to the road. Chloe and Jake followed nervously behind. Shouting for Kate and Dixie Lou, their voices carrying easily over the open spaces of the desert, the team was met within moments by the women, anxiously awaiting their return.

"Is she...?" started Kate, terrified and shaking.

Dixie Lou stepped forward and took Sunny's wrist in her hand. Checking her pulse and feeling her head, Dixie Lou gave her a cursory examination.

"She'll be okay as soon as she drinks more water and rests a bit. Got overheated, I expect. Disoriented perhaps." She noticed a small bruise on Sunny's forehead, but there were no cuts or swelling.

Kate trembled, terrified that Sunny was seriously injured. While she was comfortable stepping into emotional crises, she was useless with physical emergencies, and ashamed at her weakness. Stepping back, Dixie Lou took her shawl and placed it tenderly around Kate's shoulders. "She'll be okay," she reassured Kate. "She'll be just fine."

"Seems like she lost her dog and fell down or something," one of the men said in a whiskey voice. "We followed the dog's tracks and they led us right to her. Had that funny stuffed bear near the dog's side," he chuckled. "Sure was a strange sight!"

"Thank God," Kate sighed, relieved. She took a deep breath and resumed command. "Okay, you," she said to the scruffiest looking man, "put her in the back seat. And you," pointing to the one with a decided limp, "get in with her to hold her head. Be careful now. We'll take her home and then come back for the rest of you. Take care of Chloe. She won't hurt you. Needs water." Without looking back, Kate added, "Grab that bear too", made a u-turn and rushed to Sunny's home.

Chapter Six

When the men opened the door to Sunny's home and attempted to carry her in, they heard a peculiar sound.

Madame Luna announced in a squeaky voice, "*Hola*, come in. *Hola*, come in".

A muffled giggle was heard from the gurney. "*Hola, como esta?*" replied Sunny, the first sign of her recovery. Kate, shaken with worry, rushed to her friend's side, grabbing Dixie Lou's hand in the process.

"Let's get you to a doctor! And call your granddaughter," she insisted.

"No. Absolutely not! I am perfectly all right, just hot and tired," Sunny declared.

Madame Luna screeched loudly from her cage "Absolutely not, just hot. Absolutely not, just hot." Suddenly all three women giggled while Madame Luna chattered, whistled, and squawked, showing off as she ordinarily did when visitors arrived. She stretched her neck, fluffed her feathers and tilted her head toward the newcomers. The two men stood still, awkward, self conscious, and a bit bewildered.

After Sunny was settled on her old cozy couch with peach tea and toast, and the other two men along with Chloe and Jake were retrieved, the group huddled around to learn what had happened. In the excitement of Sunny's story telling, Kate did not notice Dixie Lou's absence.

Sunny's adventure was simple. When a coyote approached, Chloe chased it off, but soon exhausted, collapsed in the shade of the mesquite bush. "I tried to grab her," Sunny said "and held on for a while but she slipped her collar and took off like a dart. I tried to follow her in the desert. Somehow, I must have stumbled, fell, and conked my head. Don't remember too much. Guess I knocked myself out. How silly. Lost my light somewhere along the road. And my groceries I guess. Then Chloe and Jake must have come along and stayed with me."

With the mention of Jake, Kate bristled. "A dog could find her owner, but a stuffed bear? Not likely, Sunny. When your head clears you'll come to your senses, I'm sure."

Only Chloe knew the whole story. It was not to her credit alone that Sunny was saved, but to Jake's as well. Chloe made a low rumble in her throat in Jake's direction, wrinkled her soft nose and lifted her lip in a peculiar smile. Imperceptibly, Jake seemed to nod in reply.

Just as the men's discomfort with hanging out inside a proper home was becoming unbearable, Dixie Lou stepped into the living room with a tray of coffee, tea, and scrambled eggs. A bit rumpled but dressed up, in this setting and serving food on a silver tray, she was momentarily unrecognizable to her boys. She heard them mutter with approval among themselves, and she was secretly surprised and pleased.

Dixie Lou returned to the kitchen where she found a few cherries and chocolate truffles in the fridge. She added these to the offering along with sliced chili peppers and cubed cheese. Surprisingly, she even found some brandy and sampled a quick sip right from the bottle. Not particularly a drinker, Dixie Lou did enjoy a little nip when it was available. She placed the small bottle on the tray with a few glasses and then returned to the living room where she offered a glass to everyone except Bud. She put a large plate filled with dog treats out for Chloe. Unobtrusively she shook the desert dust from Jake, gave him a gentle hug and kiss and placed him back in her bag. She placed the bag on the floor next to Sunny's couch. Jake wiggled with pride and happiness. Chloe lay down next to the bag, her back against the bag, gently cuddling up to Jake.

The afternoon wore on with the group more easily warming to each other's company. The men became individuals as they talked a little about themselves. Kate, surprising herself, relaxed a bit and listened attentively without her critical ear to each guest. Jim, the man with the limp, shyly and with little detail told his story of combat and injury. His demeanor reminded Kate of Charles, but without the concomitant heartache.

Sam and Joe revealed their stories as grunts in the same unit during the Tet offensive. Most striking was their admiration and respect for the native Montagnards who hid them and stood up against the Viet Cong. "They saved our lives," Joe said matter of factly. "We couldn't have made it alone."

Bud, the oldest and most travel-worn of the four said, "My big battle was with the bottle and drugs. I still have to fight it one day at a time. Not so noble as fighting for our country though," he added humbly. His gravelly voice testified to years of alcohol and cigarette abuse but his eyes were clear and hands steady, suggesting a long but winning fight against these demons. Of the four men, Bud was the calmest, Buddha-like in nature. He stayed in the present and worked his program of sobriety and serenity with silent conviction.

Kate and Sunny, charmed and embraced by these compassionate strangers, laughed a lot and cried some as well. Only Dixie Lou was strangely withdrawn. Their stories, not new to her, triggered her own memories of nursing battered and broken soldiers during her time in Nam. She recalled being deployed to a field hospital in Pleichu. Here she rendered immediate first aid to the most horrible of wounds. Quick actions demanded quick decisions, and she often provided care under the toughest circumstances. Many times her decisions were made independent of other medical personnel when the wounded were particularly numerous. During the long night hours, her touch saved and comforted many who might not have made it until the morning medevac unit arrived. Throughout her life, however, she believed she had not done enough to save as many young soldiers as possible and felt oddly guilty that she had survived it all herself. She kept this aspect of her life tucked away, secret and private, too painful to share, along with her own debilitating heart condition.

By mid afternoon it was apparent that Sunny was tired. "Let me call your granddaughter," Kate suggested once again. She noticed Sunny was fighting to keep her eyes open as the conversation slowed.

"No, no. Don't need to worry her for nothing. I'm just fine, a little weary, that's all."

Jim's leg ached deep within the bones. His limp was more pronounced when he helped Kate carry the dishes back to the kitchen. Dixie Lou looked wan and shaky, although she continued to act with forced energy and high spirits. Bud, Sam, and Joe were restless, their need to be on the move evident. Looking over her new friends, Kate quickly suggested that she take the men home, "wherever that might be," she muttered to herself and smiled. A very strange group indeed, she thought.

"Be glad to take you to town," she said, "but Dixie Lou will have to stay with Sunny. Can't fit everyone in my car at once with all the stuff I have in the back. Jim can sit up front and stretch his leg out. You others can squeeze in wherever, okay?"

"Let me pack you each a to-go bag," Sunny offered with genuine concern but with little energy.

"No, no. You sit. I'll do it," Kate announced, happy with relief and the comfort of helping her best friend once again. She hustled into the kitchen and within moments had brown paper bags filled with odds and ends from Sunny's pantry. Dixie Lou, tired herself, simply watched and smiled.

When Kate and the boys left, Sunny turned to Dixie Lou.

"Now," she said, "Talk to me about you. And about Jake."

Chapter Seven

P icking up Jake, Dixie Lou settled next to Sunny in a soft, upholstered chair. It seemed to wrap around her slight frame, which was hidden all the more with the comfy afghan Sunny offered her. She snuggled down and tucked Jake in, leaving his head exposed for air.

"What's to tell? Just a silly old bag lady, crazy too, talking to a stuffed bear, huh?" she replied with a chuckle.

"First off, we both know you're not crazy. But I want to know if you're sick. It seems like you get breathless from time to time," Sunny observed. "I may have conked my head, don't hear well, but my eyes are just fine."

"Altitude," Dixie Lou answered. "Just altitude. Used to sea level, you know. Air's thin here. Have to get used to it."

Sunny knew this was not the whole story, but out of respect she shifted conversational gears. "All right, then what about Jake?"

"Oh Jake. Well, ya know. Jake's an old friend, a knock-around travelin' buddy for me."

Not letting her off the hook so easily, Sunny continued, "So you say but there is more to him than that. Now *tell* me about him."

Dixie Lou hesitated to reveal Jake's story. Only once before had she told someone of his significance—and that was to a mental health therapist who then dismissed him summarily. Dixie Lou hardly knew Sunny, yet she sensed Sunny's sensitivity and compassion. Could she really tell Jake's story, or perhaps part of it at this time? Trusting her own abilities to judge another's character and her tendency to engage the goodness in people, Dixie Lou decided to tell a little. She offered an abbreviated rendition of her Mama's illness, her Mama's tendency to hear voices and talk to them out loud rather than talk to Dixie Lou or her Daddy, and her ultimate death leaving Dixie Lou and her Daddy to live in parallel grief. Dixie Lou explained how her reliance on Jake for conversation grew. She relied on him solely for comfort and companionship. Jake, forever wise, offered Dixie Lou solace, guidance, and unconditional love. Sadly Daddy threw Jake away and buried himself deeper in his lonely grief.

Dixie Lou concluded her story with, "Jake's all the love Mama had for us, even if she wouldn't talk to us. I often wished Daddy could have seen this but he was too far gone into himself to believe in miracles." She paused a while, then continued. "So, anyways, that's the story. Silly, huh?"

Sunny was stunned. Such endearing hope and love in spite of tragic circumstances were remarkable. Her eye sparkled with unshed tears. If only Kate could have heard this, she thought, perhaps it might soften her natural tendencies toward distrust and cynicism.

Time passed quietly then between these two new friends. Sunny dozed on the couch while Dixie Lou and Jake snuggled in the big chair. They, too, drifted off in sleep. Chloe yipped from time to time in her sleep, feet moving, and nose twitching, reliving her great hunting adventure of the day. Only Madame Luna was alert, standing guard silently over this small group.

When Kate got back to town, Bud, Joe, and Sam wanted to be dropped off at the Main Street Bridge but Jim needed to go to the drug store. His leg was hurting terribly although he kept his complaints to himself. He simply asked Kate if she would drop him near Walgreens where he could get over-the-counter pain meds.

"Glad to take you there," Kate said, inwardly pleased to have a few moments alone with this gentle man. "In fact, I need to get some more tea for Sunny," she lied, "and I think they have some in their small food section."

Kate parked the Woodie and together they walked into the store. She felt strangely at ease with this man in spite of his appearance. They made an odd looking couple, she thought, catching a glimpse of them in the store's overhead mirror. She in her white 'wedding dress,' dirty and wrinkled, and he limping noticeably now, in old jeans and a torn t-shirt that said *Peace in Every Step*. We look like aging hippies, she mused. Well past their prime all right, but seem comfy in their place. Again, she wondered, whatever is going on with me?

After their purchases, Jim tentatively asked Kate if she would like a cup of coffee. Completely taken aback, Kate agreed with some apprehension, wondering where and how? Did this man have money to spend on her? On coffee? What's the protocol? she thought, when being asked out, so to speak, by a homeless man? The peculiarity of the situation surprised and amused her. She chuckled. "I'd love to," she replied.

Jim suggested they go to the Starbucks drive-through, get a nice latte or cappuccino, and then to the city park where they could sit and sip their coffees under the stars. It was the most romantic offer Kate ever had. She felt giddy with unaccustomed excitement.

As Kate negotiated her way to the drive-through lane, Jim placed some money in her cup holder on her console. Nothing was said, just understood. Kate ordered, got their coffees, paid, and drove to the park.

The night was beautiful, a typical star-filled sky with the moon bright over the mountains. Almost magical. They talked for hours. It was well past midnight when Kate returned to Sunny's, feeling slightly like a capricious teen-ager slipping in after a late date.

Chloe lifted her head slightly, thumped her tail a time or two, and went back to sleep when Kate entered the house. Sunny and Dixie Lou did not move but continued snoring in unison but not in tune. Kate smiled. Her heart was a little more open than it had been that morning. Confused but oddly content, she went to the guest bedroom, a tiny space within this century-old home that was snug and warm and fell upon the small bed. Within moments she, too, was snoring.

Chapter Eight

In the morning, Sunny and Dixie Lou awoke to smells of breakfast. Kate, typically appalled with the cult of domesticity, was cooking French toast, bacon, sausage, and eggs. She had slipped out early and shopped at the 24-hour store to replenish Sunny's pantry. Coffee perked and the teakettle whistled. Kate seemed to be humming slightly to herself. Sunny looked at Dixie Lou, raised her eyebrows, and smiled with curiosity and surprise.

"Breakfast!" Kate announced. "Hurry in here while it's still hot." Both Sunny and Dixie Lou *hurried* according to their particular morning pains, pleased to push their aching bodies for the sake of this wonderful early repast.

Seated around Sunny's old wooden kitchen table, the three women greeted each other with interest and concern. "Howdja sleep?" asked Dixie Lou, looking first at Sunny, then toward Kate. Each responded quickly and positively.

"Quite well" said Sunny. "In fact, very well."

"Terrific," replied Kate with a smug smile on her face. "And you?" she asked Dixie Lou graciously.

Dixie Lou, practiced in the deceit of her heart condition, responded, "just fine." She, too, smiled, amused that Sunny and Kate seemed to forget sleeping in a warm home on a soft chair with new friends was eminently more conducive to her well being than lying on the ground all night with other homeless women like herself—one eye open just in case of trouble. Little did they know she rarely slept long in one place and often slept out doors.

Dixie Lou and Kate carefully observed Sunny for signs of yesterday's accident. She seemed okay. Alert, relaxed, quite herself.

The three women chattered casually while they enjoyed their warm meal. Kate shooed the others away when they finished and cleaned up the kitchen alone with her thoughts. She had agreed to meet Jim for coffee at Starbucks later in the day and was anxiously anticipating this event. Unaccustomed to having the attention of a man, she kept her date a secret although she desperately wanted to talk about this. Was this even a date? she wondered. Well, we'll just see how this goes before sharing this news with the others, she concluded. Her excitement and hope that she could once again care for someone like Jim were tempered by her upbringing and unexplained loss of Charles. Basic trust was not in her character. And she was old now, she thought, so what would he want with her? Oddly, she never questioned what she would want with him. Preoccupied, she abruptly offered to take Dixie Lou wherever she wanted to go so that she could return home herself to prepare for the afternoon.

"Dixie Lou, would you mind staying with me a while?" Sunny asked tentatively, sensing Kate was in a hurry and Dixie Lou was not.

"Sure" replied Dixie Lou, "but I need some clothes. I'm a mess right now." Kate bit her tongue to stop herself from voicing a caustic retort. She felt herself shift a little in her usual reaction to Dixie Lou's presence. While Kate remained suspect of Dixie Lou's motives, her newfound respect for her in rescuing Sunny overrode some of her anxiety. And Sunny seemed quite at ease with her in her home. Kate put her trust in Sunny's judgment and agreed with Sunny's request for Dixie Lou to visit a while longer.

In no time, Dixie Lou and Sunny were rummaging in Sunny's closet for something suitable to Dixie Lou's needs and taste. Sunny noticed that Dixie Lou selected a heavy sweater with big pockets, even though the day was already heating up. She said nothing about it.

Kate agreed to return with a light dinner for the three of them, uncharacteristically she kissed them each goodbye, and hustled out the door, again, humming softly.

Sunny, Dixie Lou, Jake and Chloe spent the day in relaxed activities. The women chatted a lot and worked a little in Sunny's sunny flower garden, made a light lunch of peach tea and crackers with cheese, and napped in the afternoon. Dixie Lou's fragile health belied her core strength of endurance. And her helpful nature camouflaged her isolated spirit. She allowed herself to bask for a short time in the comfort of Sunny's presence. Likewise Chloe and Jake were rather inactive and at ease.

Around 4:00 p.m. Kate returned. More than ready to discuss her situation with the others, Kate blurted out almost defiantly, "I like Jim." Looking embarrassed but proud of herself, Kate sighed and turned over her unspecified dilemma to Sunny and Dixie Lou. They simply laughed, happy for Kate's romantic confusion. Together they responded, "So?"

Relieved that her friends were not ridiculing her or cautioning her against potential heartache, Kate too laughed. "Silly, isn't it?" she said. "All these years with my porch light on and the one night I don't go home, it burns out!" No more needed to be said.

Chapter Nine

The weeks passed in pleasant new routines for all three women. Kate began to meet Jim each afternoon for coffee and a chat in the park. Their conversations embraced many topics ranging from philosophical positions to the state of American politics. Rarely, though, did they border on the personal. One afternoon, a subtle shift occurred in their routine as the day grew cooler with winter approaching.

"I'm getting chilly," Kate announced awkwardly. "I forgot my shawl. I'm not much of a cook," she chattered with embarrassment, "but it is getting cold and we could at least have a little supper at my place. I live a mile out of town and I could drive you back here after we eat if you wish."

The thought of joining the world of the ordinary with dinner in a warm home, a kind female companion for whom he had loving feelings, and anticipation of a quiet and safe evening indoors overwhelmed Jim. A look of panic crossed his face.

"Never mind," Kate immediately said, noticing Jim's discomfort. Did I make another social faux pas? she chided herself. Damn, all I wanted was to be in this gentle man's company for a little longer tonight. Now what had she gone and done?

"Not tonight," Jim said, his shoulders dropping. "I have to take care of a few things first. Have to put things in order and then we'll talk, okay?" he asked with worry.

Kate, too, was cautious and so for once could put herself in another's shoes. "Sure," she said with false ease. "Another time perhaps."

Early in the morning, Jim packed his few belongings, stopped at the food pantry for coffee and a donut, made a phone call, and headed toward the bus station. The ticket to Las Vegas was $32, round trip. After fifteen hours in the bus, Jim arrived with considerable pain in his leg. He limped into the waiting room at the bus station and sat down. Eager to get away from the smells and sadness of the travelers there, but hesitant to move, he finally got up, shuffled to the phone bank and made another call. He then went to the restroom to freshen up and wait for his ride. In spite of his aching leg, he opted to wait outside, away from the smell of sour sweat, cheap liquor and stale cigar smoke inside the waiting room.

Kate, too, waited for the afternoon to arrive so she could go to the park to see Jim. Would he come as usual? Had she scared him off? Why was she like this? So pushy and needy? She tried to appear independent, but deep down wanted to have a normal relationship. She wanted to keep house, cook, make love, talk. And she knew she wanted this with Jim. As the afternoon came and went, Kate's heart hurt.

After three days of waiting for Jim and worrying about his welfare, Kate swallowed her pride and drove over to Sunny's.

Dixie Lou, Sunny, Chloe, and Jake were gathered in the kitchen where Dixie Lou was making cookies. The house was warm and smelled wonderful. Kate suddenly was angry.

"Well, what a happy little scene this is. Sweet, almost. And unreal. Life just isn't this simple," she began with her usual sarcasm. Then she crumbled with tears.

"Kate, what's wrong?" Sunny immediately asked as she put down her coffee and went to Kate's side, guiding her gently toward a chair. "Here, sit down. We'll talk."

Dixie Lou, although sympathetic, remained still.

"It's Jim. He's gone," Kate wept. "Charles reincarnated," she added with a sneer. "How could this happen again?" she said with confusion and loss. "What do I do so wrong?"

"Now, Kate, quit expecting the worst. Jim may be back right now for all you know," Sunny said.

Dixie Lou, still quiet, was quickly making her own plan.

"I doubt it. I just screwed it up again. I have no sense about how to even be in a good relationship. I always want more. Is that so wrong?" Kate asked. Tears continued to well up in her eyes and spill over her cheeks, leaving streaks in last night's make-up.

Sunny had never seen Kate so unkempt. Nor so overtly and honestly emotional about her personal life.

"Here," she offered. "Take this tissue, wash your face, and have some tea." She hoped the familiar would comfort her friend.

"All right, but I'm sick of tea. Tea for this. Teas for that. Only take it to keep you happy!" Kate replied miserably. "Do you really think he'll be back?" she asked, looking for reassurance from Sunny, her relationship yardstick. She glanced at Dixie Lou as well.

Dixie Lou, aware of Jim's history, could only trust that he would not leave Kate without an explanation. Clearly something extraordinary had occurred within him for him to simply disappear.

"I think you'll hear from him," Dixie Lou reassured Kate. "Just have faith. He's a good man and he cares deeply for you. Give him time."

"Charles was a good man too. What makes so Jim different that he'll come back?" Kate asked, somewhat assured by Dixie Lou's apparent wisdom about Jim, yet still doubtful that he would return.

As Sunny observed Kate and Dixie Lou's interaction, she, too, wondered what Dixie Lou knew that they did not. "Do you want to stay here tonight?" she asked Kate.

"No, no thanks but I want to be at home. Who knows…" she said.

"Take Jake, then, he'll keep you company," Dixie Lou ordered as she slipped Jake into Kate's large purse. "He's good for these kinds of things. Give him back when Jim returns," she concluded.

"Don't be silly," Kate replied. "Jake's good for nothing and it looks like Jim might be also," she said but without much conviction.

"Don't be too sure about that," Dixie Lou continued mysteriously. "Just do it, okay?"

"And come back tomorrow for breakfast," Sunny invited. "We'll have tea and toast with a little fruit for a change," she offered. "I'll serve your favorite prickly pear jelly and the day will unfold with sweetness for you. I'm sure of it!" Sunny declared. While Sunny seemed to minimize the worry and discount the possibility of another heartbreak for her best friend, she was eager to read Kate's tea leaves as soon as Kate left. Sunny hoped her friend's good fortune would be foretold.

Dixie Lou, however, counted on Jake to change the course of events for Kate.

"All right, I'll do it. I'll be here around eight, earlier if possible, as I know I'll be up all night with worry," Kate announced as she roughly shoved Jake deeper in her purse. Jake settled into the bottom corner of her purse, snug and warm, a bear on a mission. He was excited.

Chapter Ten

I t seemed like an hour until Jim's only child arrived, pulling up in her pearl black BMW convertible, top down. The car was custom ordered with gold and chrome accessories. The soft, black leather seats were equipped with surround sound in the head sets, and warm vibrations in the seats. Both the sound and the heat were turned up to the maximum.

"Hi Pop," greeted the young woman behind the wheel. She had her long hair, dyed black to match her car, tied up in a ponytail with a gold scarf. Her sequined dress rode well above her knees and sparkled with her enormous gold and black costume jewelry. Even her long acrylic nails were painted gold with bold diagonal black designs. Her face was unnaturally white and slashed with vivid red lipstick. Her eyes were bright but old. Had she not greeted him, Jim would not have recognized his thirty-five-year-old daughter, Tisha.

"Jump in," Tisha said. "Let's get out of this part of town. It gives me the creeps." She leaned over and opened the door from the inside for her dad. "I'll pop the trunk and you can throw your bag in there. No room up front with us," she chuckled.

Jim limped to the back of the car and sighed deeply. He hadn't seen Tisha in ten years, and he was saddened by her appearance. Expensive and gaudy was not a look suggestive of a successful professional woman. It spoke of Tisha's continuing dependence on her sex to secure that which she wanted from men. Her move to Las Vegas, to find herself, so she said, simply allowed her to sink deeper into the world of sex and drugs, reminiscent of her mother's journey. He exhaled loudly and turned to get into the car.

As Jim struggled to bend his long body and sore leg into the tiny passenger space, Tisha babbled on. "Like my car? Great, huh? Cost me nothing. I got it from a guy who likes me. Doesn't want anything from me, Pop, so don't worry. He just likes to see me happy. All he wants for himself is to be seen with me from time to time. Arm candy, he calls me. He's kinda old. So just wants a bauble on his arm and I'm it. Great, huh?" she repeated, oblivious to Jim's discomfort with the entire situation. "Where to? Want a drink? I'm just the chauffeur, so tell me where to go," she concluded.

Jim had yet to say a word.

Tisha continued, "How about the new casino? I have a suite there where you can crash after a few drinks and some gambling. We'll have a blast."

Jim wanted to run away—again. But again, he stayed with his daughter, distressed by her frenetic self-centeredness. As he looked at her profile, he saw his wife. Generational heartaches he thought.

In their world there was no room for his needs for simplicity and stability. Never room for his dreams. There was only space for his wife and daughter to run in circles after the next great fix.

"Tisha," Jim shouted over the music. "Would you please turn down the sound? And can we find a nice, quiet motel out of town where we can talk. No bells and whistles, no bright lights, just a place to have a drink, touch base, and then sleep for me."

Tisha, although anxious about why her father had turned up after so long, was relieved that she could get rid of him before the night was over. His unexpected call and request for a visit interrupted her adrenalin-filled lifestyle and the date with her old man planned for much later in the evening. She didn't want to cancel their date and piss him off, risking that he might find a younger, better-looking bauble than she. She needed him now that she was considered old in this town filled with young runaways, and she needed his money to sock away for the day she could give it all up. If she could give it up...

"Sure, Pop. How about that old Best Western we used to go to when Mom was around? Remember how we came here thinking we would get rich and happy?" As soon as the words came out of her mouth, Tisha regretted them. It dampened her mood, and she could not smoke a little pot with her Pop in the car, so she had to suffer the pain of the memory. "Nah," she said quickly. "I just remembered. I think it burned down, but there is an old Holiday Inn nearby that is clean and nice, okay? And I can park my car safely in their lot."

Jim nodded, grateful with her change in plan.

After Tisha parked the Beamer and hopped out, she noticed how difficult it was for her dad to move. She slowed down, pretending to fix her shoe, and let him catch up to her. They entered the lobby and Jim registered for a room. Then they found the bar, ordered, and sat silently looking at one another.

Jim spoke. "Tisha, I need to find your mom. Where is she?"

"Wow, thanks a bunch. No 'how are you, you look great, I missed you,' even 'I'm sorry for leaving.' You just jump to the point. Guess that tells me where I stand in your life," Tisha complained insincerely. Her nature allowed her to play the poor victim quite well with most men who wished to rescue her. It didn't work with Jim.

"Tisha, please, I need to talk to your mom. Then we can catch up with each other if you wish. Now, how can I reach her?"

"You won't like this, I guarantee you," Tisha warned. As if she knew what Jim liked and hoped for regarding her mother. Jim sipped his Scotch and pressed Tisha further. "Tish, I know your mom very well. I know what to expect. I simply need to talk to her briefly and then I'll leave her alone. Her life is hers, yours is yours, and mine is mine. Let's leave it at that. No recriminations, no regrets, no demands, no worries. Just a few words with her is all I need. Will you help me find her?"

After a few moments, Tisha nodded. She grabbed her gold lamé purse, threw some money on the table, and said, "All right, let's do this. Afterwards, the drinks are on you."

They returned to the car, and Tisha punched numbers in her Blackberry. She spoke softly when someone answered indicating she was on her way over. They drove in silence for forty-five minutes, then Tisha turned onto a gravel driveway. She grumbled as she drove across the loose stones, occasionally spinning them up on the car's undercarriage. "I usually rent a car when I come here," she commented with embarrassment.

Within a few moments they pulled up in front of a large, adobe-style home. There were lights on in every room. Tisha got out, covered her shoulders with a lacey shawl from the trunk, and started toward the main entrance. "Come on, Pop. We're here, so let's do this," she said.

Jim concentrated on controlling his limp and walked steadily toward the door. This place looks good at least, he thought. Money well spent.

When they entered, Jim and Tisha were greeted by a kind-looking woman dressed in typical nurse's fashion. She introduced herself as the night duty nurse, and without any other formality invited them to follow her to the day room. A lonely figure sat by the fire, rocking gently in her straight-backed chair. She looked content but disconnected. Her eyes were vacant.

"Hi Mom," Tisha said as she bent over and kissed the woman on her head. "Pop's here. Surprise."

There was no response from the solitary woman. She just kept rocking back and forth.

"Marilee," said Jim softly. "It's me, Jim. Tisha's dad. Do you remember?" He took her hand and kissed her palm. Marilee did not react.   Strangely, she seemed to become more withdrawn and shrunken in stature.

"Please, Marilee, please look at us. I need to talk with you. I need to know how you are. What can I do? Can I get you anything?" Jim asked as he continued to hold her hand. "Please, just a few moments, Marilee, please come back for a few moments."

"Not going to happen Pop. She's like this all the time now. Unreachable. Gone. You came all this way for nothing. Let's go, okay? I need a drink."

"You go to the car. I want to stay here a few more moments," Jim said.

"Whatever," Tisha replied as she bent over and kissed her Mom goodbye. "Don't be long." She turned and with her spike heels clicking on the floor, swiftly left the room.

Jim pulled up a chair close to Marilee, never letting go of her hand. He sat calmly staring into her face. Marilee did not move, did not even blink. She seemed waxy and posed, unable to emit any semblance of life. "Oh Marilee," Jim began. "Oh, Marilee, whatever happened to all of us. Together we drained the goodness from each other, blaming the other for our own deals with the devil.   I withdrew, stopped talking, left you and Tisha. You and she had your drugs, your escapes from the mundane. Now Tisha is rushing to get out of the fast lane with her throttle stuck on high. And you, you have retreated into a world of your own creation. And I, I just want to be free from all this. I need you to let me go. I need me to let me go on. I'm so sorry for us all but I need to move on. I love you. Always will. But I can't feel bound to you any longer."

Jim took a deep breath and sat still for a while. When he began to rise, Marilee, without a word, blinked and tenderly squeezed his hand. A sob rose in Jim's throat. He kissed her goodbye and left.

The ride back to the Holiday Inn was heavy with unspoken words between Jim and Tisha. Rather than park, Tisha pulled up to the entrance and said, "I'll pass on that drink, Pop. Have a great trip." Jim nodded, said "thanks," and went up to his room. The bus left very early the next morning and he needed his sleep. It didn't come easy for him and he awoke sluggish and disheartened. He couldn't wait to get back to Rio Rojo and Kate.

Chapter Eleven

A fter leaving Sunny and Dixie Lou, Kate drove around for a while, circling the Main Street Bridge area. It seemed so particularly dark to her that she hesitated to search on foot for Jim. Finally after twenty minutes of indecision, she parked her car along the frontage road, near the bridge underpass. Sitting quietly, eyes searching and scanning the area, she considered what she could do. Her fingers tapped anxiously on her steering wheel. Periodically she reached for the door handle but then returned to the steering wheel. She struggled with her need to flee, or remain safe within her car, terrified to enter into this potentially chaotic and dangerous situation. Another five minutes passed, and then she saw the small red glow from a lighted cigarette under the bridge. Jim admitted to enjoying a smoke from time to time, and Kate wondered if he were the lone smoker, and if she should search him out. I probly should leave well enough alone, she thought unhappily. Could get hurt, after all, if I go down there. But then again, what if it is Jim and that's his sign?

Jake, still deep in Kate's purse, began to stir. His weight shifted as Kate grabbed her purse, got out of the Woodie, and began to walk with her head held high, along the frontage road toward the bridge. Posturing always helped her to feel more in control of her emotions, but it was extremely difficult this evening to present a matter-of-fact façade.

Suddenly, a hand grabbed Kate, and a raspy voice slurred, "Hey there, lady, comin to join us?"

Kate smelled alcohol and dirt on the man and immediately tried to yank herself away. His skinny hand clutched her more tightly, pinching her upper arm, and she froze, trying to formulate a plan to get away from this obnoxious and frightening circumstance.

The man pulled her closer to him and whispered, "How about a kiss, honey. Boy, could we have fun." His breath smelled of decay, whiskey, and garlic. His body odor reeked of fever and vomit. Kate's natural inclination was to pull away from him, but her intellect told her to move closer and knee him between his legs. Before she could muster enough courage to do so, Sam appeared from under the bridge and ordered, "Let her go, take your hand off her now!" He quickly moved toward the drunk and pulled Kate out of harm's way.

"Aw, Sam, just havin some fun. What do you care?" the drunk answered. "Just want to scare her off. We don't need no women down here. And what if she's the cops or something, wanting to run us in for loitering?" he said. "Or worse yet, some do-gooder that wants to find us a home," he scoffed.

Kate was still petrified. Without thought she abruptly reached into her purse and began smoothing Jake's fur in a rhythmic manner.

The drunk, startled, backed off a little. "Whoa, lady, don't be reaching for no gun or nothing now," he whined. "Didn't mean nothing by it. I'm just an old drunk and don't know what I say."

Sam, recognizing Jake's familiar shape in Kate's purse, said "Slowly, Kate, pull out what you have in your hand and show it to this old guy. But do it real slow like, okay?" He nodded encouragement and then winked at her. Kate, teetering with worry, fear, and confusion, reached into her bag with bravado. She cupped Jake in her hand and very cautiously removed him from her purse, then thrust him into the old drunk's face. By this time, a group of six other men had appeared as silent spectators to this amusing diversion in their otherwise rather tedious lives.

The old drunk jumped back with his eyes closed, held shaky hands in front of his face, and begged, "Don't hurt me. I didn't mean nothing. I'll move along. Just leave me alone. Please lady, don't shoot!"

The spectators, recognizing Jake, howled with laughter. "Better run, old man, that teddy bear will get ya," yelled one of them.

"Hurry along now before he *scares* you to death," chided another.

Without another word, the old man stumbled off into the dark, hoping they would forget what a fool he made of himself once again.

Kate, too, was ready to run. Never comfortable with adrenalin rushes, she longed for the familiar safety of her home and bed. Sam recognized her panic and softly spoke. "Kate, it's all right. Sorry if we startled you. We saw you coming and never thought that Mickey there would cause you such a problem. These fellas are all friends of Dixie Lou and Jake. Come on now. We can have some coffee, strong stuff, not like Sunny's tea. Come, tell us what brings you to visit us for a change?"

Kate, now hugging Jake against her heart, still trembling, followed Sam to the bridge. The underpass was darker than she imagined but large and airy. Rather than a sinister sleeping area, it reminded her of a Spartan-looking but tidy campsite. There she was greeted by Joe and Bud and offered the seat of honor, a desirable spot on an old Indian blanket out of the wind. Sam handed her a tin cup filled with hot coffee.

"Jim's gone," Kate said with a sadness loaded from Charles's disappearance. "Jim's been gone three days now. Have you seen him? Is he all right?" she asked, hopeful that they had and he was all right yet afraid that he was simply avoiding her. She continued to stroke Jake and regain her composure.

Sam and Joe, faithful sentries of this small group of friends, proclaimed, "We know Jim real well, and he'll return. We may not know why or where he's gone, he's done it before sometimes, but he always ends up back with us somehow." With reassurance they added, "And now that there's you in his life, believe us, he'll be back."

Even Bud, who generally could worry only about walking along in his own path of sobriety promised, "Jim's all right. He'll be back real soon."

Kate's nerves were settling down and she began to shiver with the night air. She noticed how dirty she was from sitting on the ground and from her contact with the old drunk. Her concern for Jim somewhat abated, Kate now recognized her own uneasiness with being out of her clean and safe comfort zone and she couldn't wait to go home. Maybe Jim would be there, she thought. Maybe...

"Thanks guys. I'm really grateful to all of you. Sometimes I have trouble really trusting people and then I expect the worst. I know Jim is a great guy and wouldn't just abandon any of us. I guess I just needed to hear you say it. I feel better now. Even relieved a little," Kate said. She smiled somewhat self-consciously and hugged each of the boys. Then, offering her goodbyes, she hurried back to her car. When she sat down in the driver's seat she realized she was still holding Jake close to her heart.

Chapter Twelve

A fter Jim returned the following day, his relationship with Kate grew steadily and surely through long conversations interrupted by even longer sweet silences. He revealed his former life to her, and though ashamed of his abandonment of Marilee and Tisha, felt relieved from the burden of their care. He continued to send money to Marilee through a P.O. box and kept Tisha's number in his phone book.

Kate continued to visit Sunny but was relieved of any self-imposed guilt in spending time away with Jim, as Dixie Lou was usually there. Not officially a housemate, Dixie Lou maintained her homeless status with visits to the boys under the bridge and chats with the girls around the fire barrel on occasion. She acknowledged to herself, however, that the desert nights were becoming too cold for her to risk remaining outside through the winter.

Sunny was delighted with Dixie Lou's company and welcomed their growing dependence upon one another with Jake and Chloe for companionship. In fact, Sunny rather enjoyed hearing Dixie Lou chattering quietly to Jake and listening attentively for his response. Occasionally she thought she heard him, but with her increasing deafness she wasn't sure. Within a short time, a steady relaxed rhythm of everyday life was established among this small group.

Once a month or so, the boys came over for conversation and tea. Often they tried to teach Madame Luna new expressions, and laughed with dark humor when she squawked, "Let's lock 'n load. Let's rock 'n roll." Unspoken, each in his or her own way watched out for the others.

Bud in particular seemed to be most interested in Dixie Lou's evolving friendship with Sunny. He thought of Dixie Lou as one of the boys and enjoyed being around her. His feelings toward Sunny, however, were more complex and confusing. He was growing quite fond of her in fact. She reminded him of his first love so many years ago, before the war cloud of disillusion embraced his capacity to care deeply for another.

"Think I'll stay a while today," he commented one afternoon when it was time for the boys to leave. "I see a little step needs fixin' on the back patio, and I'll be glad to do it if you want," he offered to Sunny.

"Well, I don't know. I can fix it tomorrow myself," she stated, hesitant to admit she needed help around her place. She knew, however, that moving the patio tiles and filling in with sand to smooth their surface was difficult for her these days given the increasing arthritis pain in her back and legs. Years ago she had been thrown by her horse, broke a rib and badly injured her right leg. Traumatic arthritis settled in these vulnerable areas, and aging was worsening her condition.

"Come on Sunny," Dixie Lou implored. "Bud's a good guy and needs something to do beside actin' serene and sober all the time," she said good-naturedly. "Let him work up a sweat while we sit and watch for a change. Been a while since I've seen a good lookin' man get all hot and sweaty, how about you?"

Sunny suddenly felt a twinge of playful mischievousness. "Yep," she said. "Not too old to enjoy a hunk, are we?"

Bud blushed, speechless but pleased with this attention. They all laughed and agreed to a patio picnic once he finished the job.

Throughout the winter and spring, Dixie Lou worked with Sunny in the garden, cultivating winter pansies and ornamental cabbages. Rose bushes were pruned and nurtured. They planted early tomatoes and chili peppers. Dixie Lou noticed her clothes were fitting a little more tightly. She was sleeping better, of course, and eating well, yet she still felt empty, her life without meaning. And time's runnin' out, she worried.

Bud continued to pop in routinely and putter around Sunny's place. Often Sunny was home alone when Bud arrived. She would warmly welcome him and interrupt whatever she was doing to fix him a light snack and listen to his life stories.

"Funny," Bud remarked one evening as he prepared to leave. "I don't talk to anyone, even the boys like I do to you. I feel like I know you somehow. On some mystical level." Embarrassed he added, "Must be crazy vet thinking. Forget it. Gotta go," he said and hurried off.

In the spring, cactus began to bloom bringing bursts of reds, yellows, and fuchsia to the desert. Orange poppies covered the ground. Yucca stalks shot up with lemon-sized buds impatient to open. Even the century plants erected their tall stanchions with exquisite displays, completing their life cycles with beauty and bravado.

One mild spring evening, after a full day in the garden, Sunny paid close attention to her new friend's appearance. Dixie Lou's color was better, no longer alternating between pale gray and flushed. Her cheeks had filled in, as had her waistline. She appeared stronger, walked more steadily and tired less easily. Always cheerful, her mood was even now, without the flashes of pain previously etched in her face. Her voice was less shaky. She had been living almost full time with Sunny, moving her small backpack of possessions into the tiny guest room. Coincidentally, Sunny felt stronger also.

Bud was changing as well. By far the most reserved of the boys, he began to let Sunny into his former world bit by bit. Late one afternoon as he worked on her patio, he quietly announced, "I have some things to tell you, Sunny. Would you mind listening while I work?"

Surprised, Sunny replied, "I'd be glad to after I get us some nice iced green tea." She moved as quickly as her body would allow, eager to learn more about this gentle man. Although Sunny was a wonderful listener, used to having others share confidences with her, she felt particularly honored that Bud wished to let her into his internal world. When she returned, she sat close to Bud on her new patio chairs he made a month before. She didn't want to miss a word of what he might say. "Here you go," she offered and settled into a comfy position ready to be still and listen.

"Well," he began, "I've not always been without roots, wandering around. When I left the service, you see, I was twenty years old with an ancient soul." He took a deep breath and blew it out. "I did my share of killing and watching people die. War wasn't disconnected for me. It wasn't just a John Wayne job I was trained to do. It was a way of life for my family. And combat duty was expected. Dad was in the marines in WWII. He wouldn't talk about it, of course, but had pictures at home with him in a uniform covered with medals. He looked so proud. When I asked him to tell me about fighting, he would simply crack another beer and send me out to play. It was never discussed but I assumed that I too would follow his tradition. Well, when my low draft number came up, I enlisted to increase my chances at OCS. Got in, but had to drop out when I took emergency family leave for Mom when Dad died suddenly." He took a sip of tea, looked at Sunny to measure her response, then continued, "So, I settled for infantry training, hoping to stamp out those gooks but good. I was mad that Dad died before I could make him proud, worried sick over my mom's welfare, and trained to kill hard and fast. And I did. Over and over. But, you know, I still felt angry, and worried, and finally then…nothing. That's when I knew I had to get out. Couldn't keep killing anything that moved one day and ordered not to shoot the next. So, I simply walked off."

Bud stared off towards the mountains for a few minutes, then sighed and went on. "MIA they finally determined. I was missing all right. Missing a life dream, goals, hopes."

Sunny shifted slightly in her chair but remained quiet, attentive. She felt chilled as the sun lowered but did not want to interrupt Bud with a search for her shawl. She crossed her arms high, cupping her small breasts in her palms and tucking her fingers under her soft biceps. It helped to cradle her body warmth.

"So, I went missing. I knew where I was," he laughed, "just neglected to announce myself, I guess. Anyways, I ended up staying in Southeast Asia for almost twenty years. I bounced around. Lived with lots of women and their kids. Mostly Amerasian kids who needed protection. And young women who needed it too. They were happy with me, I was satisfied with them. No demands, no expectations, no regrets. And no commitments. And I drank whenever those old feelings of family, home, honor surfaced. Drank as much as I could to pass out and start the next day anew. Family tradition, you know," he scoffed. "Anyways, in Bangkok one night at a dirty little bar, I caught a news flash about the US on the fuzzy TV. Couldn't understand the Thai broadcaster but the pictures of the Vietnam Vets of America Conference in Washington with Oliver Stone to premier his new film, *Platoon*, got to me. I knew then I needed to return to the World, to my home world, to set things right.

Within a month, I made my way back. So, what do you think of this old deserter now?"

Sunny felt an affinity for this displaced soldier. She often imagined that Leah's father had ended up the same way. Good men, both of them, just disillusioned and confused. Too young to drink, old enough to kill, unable to vote, abandoned by their country in an unpopular and psychotic war machine, and left alone to piece it all together. She turned to Bud and said, "I think we need more tea together, don't you? But let's go in where it's warmer."

They went inside and sat in silence together for the remainder of the evening, each relaxed with the other. It was after midnight when Bud left promising to return the next morning to finish the patio work. And, perhaps. to finish his story.

Chapter Thirteen: 2005

One summer evening as Kate and Jim were sitting out on Kate's patio sipping iced tea and listening for desert night sounds, Jim said, "Kate, I'd like to get married. I know appearances are very important to you and we've been together now for some time and I think we should get legal, so to speak. Do you want to?"

Without a pause, Kate knew she did. She knew this man was special, stable, and loving. After so many years with Charles' absence, she reconciled that he was gone for good and had quietly obtained a divorce. Thereafter she struggled valiantly to seem happy and single, yet deeply longing for one more chance at a long-term relationship. Now, in her sixties she believed marital longevity depended upon emotional fidelity rather than life expectancy. She was more than ready to risk a commitment to this wonderful man and gamble that their relative good health would allow them to have many wonderful years together. Almost shyly, she quietly but firmly answered, "Of course. And thank you."

Early the next morning, Kate rushed into Sunny's house. "I have news," she announced, breathless and excited. Almost defiantly she stated, "I'm getting married," and then added, "I have to."

Sunny and Dixie Lou sat at the table cleaning peppers they had picked earlier that morning. They both squealed with surprise. "Oh my God, that's wonderful" Sunny exclaimed and quickly gave Kate a big hug.

"I knew it!" Dixie Lou stated. "Just knew it, and so did Jake."

For once Kate did not flinch with the reference to Jake's involvement but rather was a little miffed about Dixie Lou's clairvoyance.

"What do you mean, you knew it?"

"What do you mean, you have to?" countered Dixie Lou. "You're certainly too old to be 'with child'," she teased and then she and Sunny each dissolved into giggles.

Within a moment or two, Kate, confused but relieved to have shared her secret, began giggling as well. For a few seconds the three friends seemed like young girls, innocent, hopeful, and filled with anticipation and optimism.

Catching her breath, Kate went on, "Well, you know how people talk. You know how mean they can be. Saying we're living in sin or something. Can't live together but we want to. So, have to get married. Besides, we are not getting any younger and ..."

Again, Sunny and Dixie Lou broke down in giggles. Kate, so serious, and the oldest of the three of them, had no idea how silly she sounded. Sunny and Dixie Lou looked at each other, and without words, rushed to Kate, embracing her again in a big, hard hug. "Of course you have to," said Sunny, "and we will make the wedding for you."

Dixie Lou wanted to do something special for Kate so she consulted her friends at the women's shelter. It had been so many years since they were included in a social event, their opinions sought and presence solicited that their excitement and enthusiasm were magical. The girls decided to give Kate a bridal shower complete with food and decorations. They could not afford gifts, but they could lavish attention and good wishes on Kate, something she so rarely experienced in her life. They consulted the manager of the shelter, and convinced her to allow them to use the facility. The only proviso was that any homeless woman in residence could attend the afternoon event. In fact, any women hanging around the shelter that day would be invited. A phenomenal guest list!

Using white butcher paper, the hostesses covered the banged up tables and created centerpieces of carnation tissues. One especially talented woman, using lipsticks and rouge donated by others made a colorful banner wishing Kate and Jim many years of marital wonder. The shelter staff made cookies, and Sunny provided the teas.

Sunny asked Kate to pick her up and take her shopping the afternoon of the shower. Dixie Lou waited for them at the Shelter.

"I have to drop off some donations at the Women' Shelter first," Sunny exclaimed and directed Kate toward the seedier edge of town.

"Cryin out loud, Sunny, why not just send one of the boys there to drop off your things? Don't need to be seen going over there. What would people think?" Kate complained. Sunny insisted however, and Kate reluctantly complied. When they arrived, Sunny said, "Kate, please help me inside first as I'm not walking so good today. We'll get someone to come out and get my stuff." With her consistent devotion to her best friend, Kate relented with a smile and said "sure."

As the two old friends entered the shelter, an odd assortment of women shouted, "Best wishes. Surprise." Kate was overwhelmed, nearly overcome with conflicting emotions. What was this all about? she thought, with suspicion. Surprises were never good in Kate's world. "What's going on?"

Dixie Lou quickly stepped up to Kate and led her to the seat of honor, an old wooden chair covered with tissue paper carnations. She placed a thrift store veil on Kate's head, a nosegay of plastic flowers in her hand and then introduced Kate and Sunny to her shelter friends.

After some awkward moments, the small group began to giggle and share happy stories of their former love lives. Their stories transcended time and station and united them easily into a cadre of caring women. Kate felt honored to be in their presence as they welcomed her with openness and genuine acceptance. For a few short hours that afternoon, they bonded as women with hearts filled with hope and delight in the advent of Kate's marriage. Magically, Kate seemed to look younger and more secure about embracing the mysteries of love.

The wedding was set for September 30th, a particularly beautiful time of year in the Southwest. An early evening wedding was planned so that the elder guests invited could still get in their afternoon naps. Sunny and Bud were paired up as the maid of honor and best man, while Dixie Lou and Joe and Sam served as the ushers. Unbeknownst to Kate, Chloe and Jake had silent roles to play as well. Kate's granddaughter helped with the physical arrangements and Marge catered the reception. She also hand delivered invitations to the morning men's group at the restaurant. Bud passed the word along to his AA friends and Dixie Lou made sure her girlfriends at the shelter were included. With a show of self confidence, Kate declined to invite those who might gossip about her from the Old Josh congregation but did include her few faithful friends from the church's quilting bee. She asked the pastor to officiate, provided he read the wedding vows she and Jim composed. With the wedding party and guests, the number of possible participants grew steadily. Kate was amazed at how many people wanted to celebrate her good fortune. "'Probly just want free food and an opportunity to gossip," she huffed half-heartedly to Dixie Lou.

"Think so?" replied Dixie Lou. "Jake and I thought maybe they were just comin' out for an evenin's fun. Maybe want to give ya a gift or two."

More often than not these days when Jake was mentioned, Kate did not bristle. Small concessions were made as the wedding date drew near. Her happiness overrode her embarrassment and she became an aging but blushing bride-to-be. Jim, quiet, steady, and loving, supported Kate in every plan and detail of their big day. The boys, amused but delighted in Jim's ability to let go of the war legacies of disillusionment and disbelief, allowed a little guarded hope to enter their own consciousness. Bud, in particular, began to *truly* entertain the concept of a higher power. And the idea that some things were simply meant to be.

The wedding was held in the old gazebo on the plaza. It was decorated with desert wildflowers and ribbons. A small table was set up as the altar upon which two white candles burned alongside a chalice of wine. The wedding vows were written on parchment and placed within a brocade-covered folder, a gift from Sunny's granddaughter.

The evening was warm and comfortable, the sky sprinkled with brilliant stars and a full moon offering natural light to this extraordinary event. Joe and Sam seated the guests on folding chairs in front of the gazebo while Dixie Lou took pictures on a throwaway camera she purchased at the Dollar Store. She seemed especially content to remain an observer to this event.

A small group of elderly musicians, some of whom breakfasted at the men's table, with unsteady and painstaking moves, presented Kate and Jim with a lovely wedding march. Sunny and Bud, with Chloe and Jake nearby as witnesses waited at the altar.

When Kate saw her friends, and their assorted pets and companions, she cried. Looking at Jim, her heart quickened and opened, allowing a wellspring of love to enter.

How had she been so lucky? she wondered. Is this truly magic or a trick of her aging mind, a terrible delusion that with the next breath would dissipate and disperse into the star filled night like so many purple thistles in flight. Could she truly believe that Jake could talk? And that she could really trust in love?

Chapter Fourteen

A nother year passed with Sunny, Dixie Lou, and their pets settling into their small world as if they were life-long companions and roommates. Madame Luna learned some new phrases, possibly at Jake's prompting. She seemed to have developed a Brooklyn accent. Chloe slept most of the day and evening yet alerted whenever company arrived. She embraced Dixie Lou and Jake within her circle of responsibility, watchful and protective in spirit if not in body.

The phone rang early one morning, jarring Dixie Lou awake. Sunny, sleeping on her good ear, heard nothing. It was Kate.

"Kate, what is it?" Dixie Lou said.

"Sorry to call so early but I need some advice. Jim wants to have his daughter come out here and I'm not sure that's a good idea. I…"

Interrupting her, Dixie Lou assumed command and gently ordered, "Get over here right now. I'll wake Sunny and we'll have tea. We bought some scones yesterday that Marge made so we can warm those up too."

"Tea?" huffed Kate, and then laughed. "This calls for coffee for me at least. Maybe even Irish coffee is in order. Be right over." She quickly hung up, pulled on her old jeans and turtleneck sweater, and warmed up the Woodie. In no time she was pulling into Sunny's driveway.

By the time Kate arrived, Sunny and Dixie Lou were at the kitchen table sipping their morning tea. Eggs, bacon and scones awaited in the warming oven. They greeted Kate with a big hug and ushered her quickly to her favorite place at the table. Jake occupied the fourth chair as usual.

"As you know," Kate began, "Tisha is quite a worry to Jim. Since his visit to Vegas last year, they have been talking once a month or so. After each conversation Jim becomes pensive, withdrawn. I try to talk to him but he shuts me out. So you can imagine my feelings toward Tisha at this point. An intruder. An interloper. I'm almost jealous of her relationship with Jim. I know it's not right to feel this way, but I do." Kate looked ashamed and forlorn, her new and safe world with Jim threatened, her sense of love and trust tested.

Sunny, ever compassionate, offered, "Kate, please don't chastise yourself so. It's natural to feel worried about an unanticipated intrusion into the life you and Jim have been establishing. While your circumstances may be complex, your goodness will guide you in this. And trust in Jim. He's with you no matter what."

"Perhaps you didn't hear me Sunny," Kate said with impatience. "I don't *want* her to come. I want things to remain just perfect with Jim and me. I'm too old to become a stepmother and too selfish to give up her father."

Dixie Lou, appreciating Kate's dilemma, stepped in with an idea. "How about letting this drama unfold naturally? If Tisha wants to visit, have her manage her own accommodations. Keep your routine with Jim and support her independence. Let Jim determine that he must keep her at arm's length for her sake as he did in the past."

"Do you really think so? Do you think it will simply work itself out?"

Jake wiggled in assent. Kate was not impressed.

The following Wednesday, Tisha arrived. She flew in first class, rented a BMW convertible, and with the top down in spite of the chilled air, breezed into town with her now red hair tied up in a ponytail with cobalt blue ribbons to match the car. As she pulled up to Jim and Kate's place, she blew the horn several times before hopping out and rushing to ring the doorbell.

"Wow," she said as Kate opened the door before her finger left the bell. "You're Kate. Hi. I'm Tisha. Where's Pop?"

"Your *Dad is* at the store. Come in," Kate said as she examined the young woman at her door. Tisha's ensemble consisted of a cobalt blue jumpsuit, flashy silver plated necklaces and dangling earrings, and silver high heel sandals. Her nails were blood red and matched her lipstick. In Rio Rojo, she appeared to be in costume, a caricature of a Vegas hooker. In Vegas she appeared as she was, and no one gave her a second glance.

"Nice place you got," offered Tisha. She looked around, unaware of Kate's disdain of her presence yet alone her opinion. "Must have cost you quite a bit to decorate like this," she said looking at the fine art Kate had collected over the years. "But Pop's money sure helps out, huh?"

Fortunately Jim walked in before Kate could snap back with one of her famous retorts. "Hey," he said, and gave Tisha a self-conscious hug. "Guess you two have been getting acquainted. Kate, how about some coffee, okay?"

"Coffee? After that trip I just had I need a drink. A martini would do," Tisha suggested. She flung her silver lamé purse on the couch, kicked off her heels and plopped down, tucking her legs under her like a kid. She almost appeared vulnerable, a trait that served her well with the men in her life. Kate recognized the ploy for what it was and huffed into the kitchen to make coffee.

"Sorry Tish. We just have coffee. You can get a drink in the hotel bar where we got you a reservation. It's the nicest La Quinta in town. After some coffee and a little chat, we'll give you directions since you must be exhausted and wish to rest up for tomorrow."

"I thought I was staying with you Pop. What's up? And what's going on tomorrow? I just want to sleep most of the day and then check out this town's nightlife. Maybe you and me can do it together and get some quality father-daughter time in." Tisha's good nature and naiveté about family relationships enabled Jim to forgive her insensitivity to Kate.

"Look Tisha, Kate and I are a married couple, and we plan our days together. We'll be glad to show you around in the afternoon. In fact, we'd like you to meet some of our friends," he said leaving little room for discussion.

"Oh. Well, okay then. I guess I'll go out alone tomorrow night. Can't stay past Friday so have to get it all in at once," she laughed. Little did she know she could get it 'all in' in a few hours in Rio Rojo.

Kate, having regained her composure, graciously entered the living room with a tray of coffee, warm sopapillas, and honey. The trio chatted easily for an hour, and then abruptly Trisha decided to get to her motel. The conversation was becoming too mundane for her, and her need for excitement was surfacing. They made their plans for the next day and said their goodnights. Kate was glad to see Tisha go. So was Jim.

At 2:00 the next day, Jim and Kate picked up Tisha and headed to Sunny's. Initially Tisha wanted to drive the Beamer but Kate prevailed by indicating that Sunny's road was rough and rugged, more suited for the Woodie than for a sports car. Tisha had had a good rest and was cheerful about meeting her dad's friends, an event she had never experienced before with him. In fact, it was curious to her to even consider her father as any one other than the bad person who abandoned her mother and her. She never considered how he might be as a man, a spouse, and a friend to others.

Dixie Lou, familiar with Jim's story, decided to test the magic of their intimate circle of friends and invited the boys to meet Tisha as well. When Kate parked the Woodie, and Tisha opened her door, she saw five people, a large bushy dog, a stuffed teddy bear held by a very little old lady and a noisy parrot in a cage on the patio waiting to greet her. It was overwhelming.

At once all five people said "welcome, hello, come in" and the bird added "*hola, coma esta?*" With a nervous laugh Tisha smiled cautiously and followed Kate and Jim into the small adobe house. There she was greeted more intimately with hugs and hellos. Such a warm and genuine welcome was uncommon in her world of flash and façade. She was conflicted about her reaction, longing for inclusion yet suspicious of everyone's motives.

"Write your address down on a piece of paper for me, will ya?" asked Dixie Lou. "Maybe we can talk that way from time to time." Tisha complied.

The afternoon passed quickly with Tisha as the center of attention and the group genuinely interested in her as a person. Each wanted nothing from her, except Jake who somehow wound up on her lap. Her initial anxiety and discomfort was offset by her repetitive stroking of Jake's kinky fur. That night Tisha returned to her hotel room and remained there, disinterested in pursuing the town's nightlife. She had a lot to think about. She left the next day after a phone call to her dad and a thank you to Kate.

Chapter Fifteen

One morning Dixie Lou announced, "Sunny, why don't we go on a trip? Take Chloe, Madame Luna and Jake and just go somewhere." Feeling better than she had in years, her wanderlust returned and she needed to explore, to find something meaningful, whatever it was.

For that first year after Dixie Lou came home from Nam, she had bounced around in search of work. Sometimes she worked as a fill-in nurse at Maimonides Hospital but was uncomfortable with all the administrative paperwork she found herself doing instead of the hands on nursing she so loved. She also had a difficult time caring for those who seemed to *enjoy* the attention of medical personnel in the face of minor medical concerns. Dealing with the children broke her heart again and again. Occasionally then she would work at the VA where she felt most comfortable but guilty, somehow, that she was the caregiver rather than the caretaker. She lived in a cheap hotel, sharing a bathroom with others on the floor. She needed little social interaction, but she occasionally bumped into Joe and Sam on the streets and even visited with them periodically in the Majestic Theater. Her visits with her father decreased as he aged and became even more melancholy and withdrawn. She was alone with Jake and once again drew comfort from his presence.

"You know, Jake, I just don't feel right," she had confided. "I'm restless. Feel the need to move on but I don't know where to or why. And I can't always work in hospitals what with my lungs and all. I can't lift, don't have the stamina to do the heavy work and gotta be careful about infections. What do you think? Shall we simply head west, where it might be warmer? And easier to get lost? Maybe find our way during the trip, huh?" Jake had agreed cautiously.

Dixie Lou's need to do something meaningful and her sense of disconnection were resurfacing and she had to address this once again.

Sunny also felt good. At sixty-six, she felt alive and energized with the company of Dixie Lou and Jake. She missed Kate's frequent visits but comforted herself with the thought that Kate was softening with love and life with Jim. They came over occasionally but often were in a hurry to return home to focus on one another and their budding lives together.

Always up for adventure Sunny replied, "Where to? And how? You still don't drive well enough for us to get anywhere safely," she teased.

Dixie Lou smiled with secret delight that Sunny so easily considered this idea. "I've been thinkin'. What if we took a train across country to Brooklyn? Could see the sights, meet people. See where I grew up. Like to visit my mama's grave, too. She's buried in a little Jewish cemetery, Maimonides, on Jamaica Avenue. I'd like to say a Kaddish prayer for her."

Completely surprised with Dixie Lou's revelation of faith, Sunny immediately agreed. "I do have a little extra money since we've been sharing expenses. And my granddaughter gave me some for my birthday. Wanted me to do something special with it anyways." Muttering under her breath, she started to add up her savings but Dixie Lou interrupted her.

"Don't need to worry 'bout money. Have quite a bit now." Again surprised, Sunny waited to hear more.

"You see, daddy died a little while ago. Lived long and hard. He developed mesothelioma from working around asbestos in the shipyards. Ended up in a nursing home, sad, alone, and angry. When he died, left a note about me. Said to find me and give me whatever he had. It took them this long but finally they tracked me down through my social security records and I got some money. So let's just go and have fun, okay?"

Over the next several weeks, Sunny and Dixie Lou spent time at the library, surfing the Net for travel deals and accommodations. Sunny's granddaughter, ever the overseer of her nana's well-being, insisted that they get a berth on the train and travel first class. She made arrangements for the animals and connected them with a driver who would take them wherever they chose while there and report back nightly to her on their welfare. She also gave her grandmother a cell phone with an afternoon of instructions to both Sunny and Dixie Lou on how to use it. It was a prepaid, disposable phone, and Dixie Lou was particularly interested in it.

The night before their departure, Sunny and Dixie Lou went to Kate and Jim's for a goodbye dinner. The boys and Marge were invited. When Marge arrived, she handed Kate a dish wrapped in aluminum foil. "Dessert," she said. "Sopapillas, home made." Not quite in keeping with the meal's Italian theme, Marge's renowned puff pillows drenched in honey were delicious and welcomed.

"Put them on the counter" Kate ordered. "And let's eat."

The meal was better than usual, as Kate had been practicing her cooking skills and Jim, his comfort with becoming a host. They served a delightful tossed salad with raisins and pine nuts, garlic bread twists, and manicotti with marinara sauce. Wearing red and white aprons, together they made a complementary twosome.

With after dinner coffee and tea, the small circle of friends relaxed in each other's company, reflecting over their year of changes and developing relationships. "We have something for you," Bud announced. Awkward, he thrust a pair of theater tickets at Sunny and continued, "These are from all of us." Deeply touched, Sunny and Dixie Lou looked at each other and smiled. The night ended early, filled with laughter and anticipation.

At six o'clock the following morning, the traveling companions boarded their train. The ride across country was long but pleasant. Chloe slept most of the way in the berth, perfectly content. On the occasional stops, Sunny walked her outside but she was eager to return to the comfort of her sleeping quarters. Madame Luna felt a little distressed with the constant motion of the train but practiced "All aboard" with finesse. She enjoyed the stimulation of the changing scenery and the occasional visits from other passengers taken with her beautiful gray coloring and extraordinary maroon tail. She was quickly learning new phrases and new accents, a challenge welcomed by this gifted creature. Jake, although quiet, was ever present and ever observant.

"Dixie Lou, I'm about ready to get to the city, aren't you?" Sunny moaned on the fourth day. "I don't like to complain, but I need to walk a bit. Miss my morning exercises. Need to stretch out these old bones."

Beside herself with anticipation, Dixie Lou replied, "Can't wait to hear folks talk like me. Look like me, even act like me. Love Rio Rojo but miss the city's pace. Miss the smells. Food cookin' on the streets. Always somethin' going on. People all around. Some actin' crazy even and nobody notices. Crowds with their anonymous connections. Don't get me wrong——I love my connections back home. Just 'ppreciate the differences in big city life. Can't wait. We're almost there."

The train pulled into the station only a few hours late. Their driver, Marcos, was waiting patiently for them. He was tall, dressed in a dark suit, shiny black shoes and a chauffeur's hat, and holding a sign up with their names on it. With his slender frame and dark hair, his appearance against the white tile wall of the train station was quite impressive. He spotted Sunny and Dixie Lou long before they saw him. Hard to miss two little old ladies with a dog, a talking bird, and suitcases with a teddy bear on top of one of them, he said to himself and stepped up quickly to help.

"Welcome to the Big Apple," he said with a slight bow. "I am Marcos, your driver and protector. You have no worries from me. Let me assist you."

Sunny and Dixie Lou struggled to keep from tittering. Marcos appeared very gallant with a hint of old world Hispanic charm. His countenance and accent were familiar to them. They felt special and strangely young again. They had come all the way to New York City and felt right at home.

"Thank you," said Dixie Lou, stepping up as leader of this little caravan. "I'm Dixie Lou, formerly of Brooklyn, now a resident of the Southwest. And this is Sunny, my very good friend." Eyes sparkling she nodded toward Chloe and said, "Her dog, Chloe and bird, Madame Luna. My buddy on top of that suitcase is Jake. And we're all ready to have a great time, so let's go!"

Marcos, pleased with the easy manner of his charges, settled them into his limo, made sure they were comfy, and then headed toward the Marriott, assuring them they would be there in no time.

Sunny was too excited to settle down into a hotel room. "Can't we see some of New York now? I've never been here before. Never been in a limo either. I feel like a movie star or something, like someone extraordinary. And I want people to look at us and wonder who we are as we drive around," she pleaded, feeling embarrassed.

Both Marcos and Dixie Lou smothered their chuckles. Marcos eased into traffic and quickly became one of many limos driving through the city.

After a half-hour of stop-and-go driving, Sunny was ready to unwind at last. While she desperately wanted to experience every moment without rest, her body refused. Her eyes heavy, her mouth open, she began to doze off.

Dixie Lou whispered to Marcos, "I think we'd better get to the hotel now while we have a chance. She'll run us ragged if we let her." Looking at her in the rear view mirror, Marcos nodded, smiled, and smoothly navigated through traffic arriving at the hotel without incident. Arrangements were made for him to pick them up at 10:00 the following morning when they would go to Maimonides Cemetery.

Chapter Sixteen

"Better take a sweater," Dixie Lou suggested, as she and Sunny got ready in the morning to venture into the city. "And a hat. It can get chilly with the wind coming off the water. And I'd like to walk around my old neighborhood, if you're up to it. Marcos can wait for us at the end of the block. Need to get out of the limo to really get the feel of my old home. Will give Chloe a little exercise as well."

Jake, extremely excited, could not be still, his fuzzy little body trembling with anticipation. Dixie Lou placed him in the pocket of her oversized sweater, slipped her money into another pocket, tucked some in her bra and was ready to go in no time. Sunny watched Dixie Lou's 'city transformation' with amazement. Almost a bit bossy like Kate, she thought. Wish Kate was here now to see this. Dixie Lou's certainly not a crazy bag lady Kate thought, even though she does have a talking teddy bear in her pocket. For a quick second, Sunny acknowledged that she too thought she could hear Jake speak. Wow, she thought. Am I getting caught up in the magic of this city? Or just going a bit dotty myself? Out loud she said "Well, Chloe, hear that? Are you ready for our big outing? I sure am!" Chloe's eyes brightened and her tail wagged furiously.

Marcos called from the limo to announce he was nearby. "I have coffee, tea, and lattes for you. Also double-baked almond croissants from the Bountiful Baking Company. A must! And a new walking stick for Sunny. Do you need anything else?" he asked.

"Geez," Sunny replied. "Not at all. How thoughtful and how wonderful. We're all ready."

The trip from the Marriott to the cemetery did not take long. Dixie Lou was unusually withdrawn. Even Jake was still. Sunny was struck with the number of park-like cemeteries they passed by on their way to Jamaica Avenue. Jewish, Catholic, Lutheran, unending beautifully kept lawns with exquisite monuments packed together. An ecumenical community in solemn tribute to generations of loved ones. The green lawns, shiny monuments, and coiffed flower beds were in stark contrast to the wind-swept, open desert landscape of the cemeteries back home.

"Please stay in the limo if you're cold," suggested Dixie Lou. Sunny watched as the wind blew Dixie Lou's wispy hair about as she stepped from the car. She pushed it back into her hand-me-down crocheted cap she had on, pulled her sweater tight around her body, wrapped her shawl on top and began the slight ascent to her mama's headstone. Suddenly her appearance reminded Sunny of their first encounter. She seemed small again, not robust and healthy looking.

"No, no. I'll go with you if you want." Sunny wished to support her friend but was also curious about Dixie Lou's mama. She thought perhaps Dixie Lou would talk more about herself prompted by the sight of her mama's grave. She, too, stepped gingerly from the limo, adjusted her new walking stick and followed Dixie Lou.

Marcos hung back outside the limo, watching the two old ladies make their way onto the grassy hillside. Chloe lay at his feet.

"Here it is," said Dixie Lou. The two friends stood side-by-side, quiet together for a few moments. They shivered a little but were not really cold.

Dixie Lou broke the silence. " 'Hannah Mae Klein. Born September 6, 1914. Died September 30, 1947. Beloved mother and wife.' My aunt Rachel took care to see that these arrangements were made. She came from South Carolina where she and Mama grew up. Only Jewish family in town. Daddy couldn't do it. He was too deep in grief."

Softly Dixie Lou began to chant, *"Yitgadal v'yitkadash shmei raba…"* The wind stopped as she continued with the prayer for the dead. It seemed that Jake softly said "amein." So did Sunny. With a large sigh and a few moments' pause when the prayer was finished, Dixie Lou was ready to leave.

"Thank you," she said to Sunny. "Haven't been here since the funeral when I was very little. Been remiss in saying Kaddish prayers. Needed to remember and say a few words privately with mama now as I'm getting older. Closer to her, you know. Thank you." Sunny, taken aback with this revelation, simply squeezed her friend's hand and they returned to the limo arm in arm.

With apparent relief and light-heartedness, Dixie Lou directed Marcos to Columbia Street off Atlantic Avenue. "My old neighborhood was near the shipyards," Dixie Lou offered. "Daddy was a longshoreman. Native New Yorker. Met Mama in Charleston when he went there to work the ships once. Anyways, he used to go down to the docks at 3:00 A.M. every day, shape up, and wait for the boss to pick the day's crew. Sometimes he was home in an hour. Others he was gone all day and evenin'. Never knew exactly when he'd be around." Dixie Lou slipped into memory and recounted how her mama planned their Shabbos meal on Fridays but often sundown arrived before her Daddy did. "Didn't matter much to him, he wasn't Jewish. But it mattered to Mama. I think that might be when she began talking out loud to herself. Prayed the Sabbath prayer but seemed to go on a bit, offerin' our best meal to imaginary guests. Jake and I were included, of course, and we joined in quite matter of factly. Daddy never did understand how much this meant to Mama," she said with resignation but without bitterness. "Gave us a chance to be close together for a while, ya know."

When they neared Dixie Lou's block, her spirits lifted again. Her eyes sparkled and a smile of nostalgia softened her lips.

Parking at the end of the street, Marcos could keep a good eye on his charges. They were easy to spot—-Dixie Lou with her oversized sweater, Jake in her pocket with his head poking out, and Sunny hobbling along with Chloe and her walking stick. Both women, although obviously elderly, moved with confidence and strength. Women with a mission, whatever it is, he mused. He would keep a good watch on them though as the area was a little seedy. He would make sure they were safe and had their cell phone number to call if they got out of sight.

As Dixie Lou and Sunny walked along, in no time a few homeless street people recognized Dixie Lou.

"Dixie Lou, Jake," they called out to her. "Over here, come and talk a while with us." They appeared from alleys, doorways, and storefronts. Many shuffled along, hurrying to catch up to Dixie Lou. They gave her soft hugs and acknowledged Jake as well.

"Howdaja like the West?" several asked.

"Have ya both been well?"

"We've missed you."

Many welcomed Sunny to the Big Apple with sincerity and graciousness as if they were to become her personal tour guides and ambassadors of good will. Not much was said about Dixie Lou's appearance but quiet approval was felt. Dixie Lou asked about various old friends to discover some had passed away while others ended up in the County Home. Surreptitiously she slipped some money into each hand and kissed each wrinkled cheek. From deep within her pocket, she pulled out baggies containing Big Mac coupons, tea bags, granola bars, band-aids, aspirin, and small tubes of antibacterial ointments. A white note card was included with her name and cell number. "Call if you need help" was inscribed. She passed out a few disposable cell phones she had purchased in Wal-

Mart back home, safety links to be used among them. Jake seemed to say "Be well" to each gentle soul as they moved along. After an hour both travelers were tired so they said good-bye to Dixie Lou's friends and motioned Marcos to pick them up.

Sunny had a million questions to ask her friend but Dixie Lou was pensive. Sunny decided their conversation would occur later after a warm dinner and rest at the Marriott. They returned to the hotel, ordered room service, put on their flannel nighties and settled in for the remainder of the day. Chloe was tired as well but Jake seemed animated and unsettled. The sounds, sights, and smells of his old neighborhood were quite overwhelming and he was scwurmy with excitement. It had been quite a day of mysteries and surprises.

Although Sunny waited patiently for the chance to discuss the day's events with Dixie Lou, she fell asleep very early and slept soundly throughout the night. Dixie Lou, on the other hand, was awake well into the early morning hours turning ideas over in her mind. By morning she was ready to put her plan into action.

Chapter Seventeen

Sunny awoke feeling rested and eager to get on with the sight-seeing she and Dixie Lou had planned. She looked over at Dixie Lou sleeping with her night light on. She quietly went to the bathroom, brushed her teeth and hair, and dressed in her casual cotton slacks and knitted sweater that didn't quite match. Always a bit of a flower child, Sunny's disregard about the approval of others was becoming exaggerated as she aged and with Dixie Lou's unstated influence, she was becoming even less concerned with convention and more comfortable with herself these days.

Dixie Lou was stirring under her covers when Sunny re-entered the bedroom.

"Good morning," Sunny said. "Wow, I feel great. Ready to go out and shop, eat, do all the tourist things I've never done. We better call Marcos and get ready. How about if we find a great diner to have breakfast at, you know, like the ones in the movies? After that we can go on the Staten Island Ferry, see the Statue of Liberty, visit Ground Zero, have lunch at that Italian place by Rockefeller Center, have a little wine maybe too, huh?" she chuckled. "Then, a small rest back here, and…"

"No, Sunny. We can't do this today. Some things I gotta figure out. Have to get the word out to all my street friends. I need to talk to them more. So today, have to shop a bit at a discount store, get some necessities, and get ready to see them," she declared quietly.

"What are you talking about?" Sunny asked, confused. A meeting with street people was never a part of their plan. "If there's a few more people you want to see, that's okay. Marcos can take us over like yesterday."

"No," Dixie Lou stated. "Need to see the down-and-outers. Those folks who are alone, sick maybe, scared. Those who stay 'under', don't come out at all except at night. Then they search for food, a spot to camp for the next day, and a warm place to rest. They ask for nothin'. Kinda like nomads. On the move, searchin', lookin', survivin' somehow. Gotta talk to them."

Sunny was alarmed and scared. Her good open nature, spirit of adventure, and compassionate character were suddenly being tested. Embracing a humanist point of view in Rio Rojo was being challenged in The Big Apple. To go out at night, in the city, in search of down and out street people frightened her. This was not in their travel plans when they considered this trip.

After a few long moments of silence, Sunny said with some reservation, "All right, Dixie Lou, if you must, you must. We can have Marcos drive us around and …"

"'Fraid not, Sunny. No way a chauffeured driven limo is going to travel safely where I need to go. Would be an open invitation to get mugged, or worse. I'll just head out on foot and find my way to a good meetin' place and wait for others to show up. I know who can send the word out for me."

"But Dixie Lou," Sunny pleaded, "you're not so young anymore, and you've been away for a while. It's not safe out there. Who knows what could happen?"

Dixie Lou grinned sadly. "I know only too well what can happen. Don't worry. Been there lots of times myself and can make my way around okay. Won't be long. Maybe a coupla hours. I have to do this," she said with conviction. "I have to."

Sunny took a deep breath and slowly exhaled. "Then I'm going with you. Chloe too and Jake. And my walking stick for protection if we need it. What if we took Marcos too? Dirtied him up a bit. Got rid of his shiny patent leather shoes. We'll all go. You're not going alone!" she said with uncharacteristic bossiness and a bit of bravado. Dixie Lou smiled, hugged her friend, and said, "Glad you feel that way. I wanted company and I'm sorry I'm messin' up our original plans for today but, well, you'll see. I have no other choice."

Sunny and Dixie Lou then spent the early morning hours eating a light breakfast in the hotel restaurant, arranging for Marcos to take them shopping, and without conversation, going about their morning activities. Sunny felt queasy, her breakfast sitting hard on her stomach. Strangely, she was annoyed in the restaurant when she saw other diners picking at their meals or gorging themselves at the breakfast buffet. The trash containers were full of wasted food and the well dressed guests were impatient to get done with eating so they could get on with their touring. All at once, Sunny's wonder at the magic of this trip to the city was threatened. She had little to say to Dixie Lou until Marcos arrived to pick them up.

When the women were settled in the limo, with their mid-morning lattes and croissants, Sunny choked back a scream. The disconnect, the incongruity, the enormous difference between their everyday life and what they were about to observe later that evening was crushing.

"Wait, Dixie Lou, we have to talk. I need to know what we're doing. I'm embarrassed to admit that while I love you and trust you, this is a bit beyond my comfort zone. I'm scared." She paused. "But I'm going, so what is this all about?"

Although Marcos was expected to be an invisible observer, he could not help but react to the undercurrent of dissension between Sunny and Dixie Lou. He hesitated to start the limo, waiting instead for a lead from one of his charges,

"Okay, Sunny, Marcos," Dixie Lou began, "I do need your help. I called one of my friends on her new cell and told her we need a meetin' place and a chance to talk with as many of the river rats as possible. She's puttin' the word out. We have to get to the riverbank near the shipyards. 'Round 9:00 and just settle in and wait to see who comes. Need to blend in too so have to get some clothes that are suitable. Sorry, Marcos, we need your help too but you'll have to get dirty, okay?"

Marcos grinned, agreed, and even seemed excited about this strange request by these unusual old women. Yesterday's adventure along Columbia Street secured his respect for his entourage, including the dog and funny teddy bear. And he was well aware of his responsibility for taking care of all of them. Whatever Miss Dixie and Miss Sunny wanted he would try to provide, he proudly told himself.

"Oh, by the way, Marcos, no calling my granddaughter now!" Sunny ordered.

Marcos, surprised, smothered a groan.

"Oh, I know you report in each night. I know she wouldn't let me out of her sight without a link through you. But you're to tell her nothing about tonight's plans. I'll fill her in when we get back. Just say that we are going out for a little stroll. "

"Yes, Miss Sunny, but what if she asks where?" Marcos stated.

"Marcos, Marcos, you know how to smooth talk a young lady. And how to respect your elders. I know you can figure this out. And keep in mind, your job is to be our driver and protector, just like you said, and not simply keep my granddaughter happy with silly little nightly reports about us. We weren't born yesterday, you know. We can take care of ourselves quite well." Sunny said, with unusual indignation.

What's happening to me? she wondered. I'm not bossy like this. Nor do I look for danger and difficulty. If it comes to me, I can handle it. I think. But to search out trouble, at night, in the dark, along the river with my friend, my dog, and her bear is bizarre. Oh well, the joy in getting old is that I can do the unnatural and it appears normal.

"Let's get going now and get our shopping done," Sunny concluded out loud, hugging Chloe more tightly around her huge neck. Chloe's large tongue licked her cheek affectionately.

Chapter Eighteen

Marcos drove to the largest discount store near the Marriott. After he dropped Dixie Lou and Sunny off near the entrance, he parked and waited in the limo with Chloe and Jake while they shopped. Aware the evening's adventure could be dangerous, Marcos began to consider how he could most safely care for his little group. He was growing quite fond of all of them and felt personally compelled to keep them safe.

Sunny was overwhelmed and felt small inside the giant store. It was noisy, crowded, and seemed unending. The pace of the shoppers seemed frenetic. Why, it would take us hours to shop here, she worried. She turned to Dixie Lou and confessed, "I'm lost. How do we shop here? What do we buy?"

"Just follow me for a while and get the feel for this place," Dixie Lou offered. Once Dixie Lou explained the necessities she wanted, Sunny quickly embraced the idea of helping others by respecting *their* needs and went off alone to buy cigarettes, junk candies, Ramen Noodles, crackers, Spam, and other sundries relevant to life on the street. She included travel size toothbrushes and toothpaste, handi-wipes, soap and several packages of small washcloths and towels. She picked up her usual pace and felt like her old spry self again.

Soon Sunny discovered small fleece throws on sale which delighted Dixie Lou as she recalled how important small but warm wraps were to those who had no homes. Sleeping under the overhang of a warehouse on the wharfs or near the metal grill of an exhaust duct in the city was insufficient for warmth during the winter months. A wrapped shawl, blanket, or throw significantly helped to stave off frostbite or even death by exposure. Dixie Lou's find included small finger lights, like Sunny's, disposable pre-paid phones, and woven shoulder bags big enough to hold considerable personal possessions.

In no time, Marcos spotted the women pushing two overfilled shopping carts toward the limo. He opened the truck and jumped out to help pack the purchases inside.

"Uh, no Marcos. Please put what we bought inside with us. We have to get the carts in the trunk somehow. Both of them," Dixie Lou stated matter-of-factly.

Marcos hesitated, well aware of the scene they might create, his livelihood and freedom endangered by such a theft. Yet, he knew to openly disagree with his charges would be useless and call greater attention to passersby. Quickly and quietly he suggested that he would get the carts after he took Dixie Lou and Sunny back for their rest. He also knew that he had to talk to his cousin who could find a reliable friend with an old beat-up car who would pick them up later and drop them off near the wharf. This friend would also secure two shopping carts for his little old ladies.

Satisfied with this plan, Dixie Lou directed Marcos to the City Mission Thrift Shop. There, Sunny and Dixie Lou donated the clothes they were wearing in exchange for warm and worn coats, sweaters, shoes, socks, and jeans. Sunny picked out a warm scarf for her neck and Dixie Lou selected an oversized coat under which she planned to wear her sweater with Jake safely tucked in the pocket. Marcos kept his chauffeur suit and cap but chose old tattered jeans, a hooded sweatshirt, black skullcap, and dark tennies. He donated a pair of slacks, sweater, and shirt he kept in the trunk for off-duty activities. Satisfied that they all looked street-weary, they returned to the hotel where they received particularly directed stares as they made their way across the lobby to the elevators. Heads held high, Dixie Lou, Sunny, Jake and Chloe marched along muffling giggles and hiding grins.

While Sunny napped, Dixie Lou called a few women to whom she had given cell phones. She was told to look for a Puerto Rican woman named Juana. Juana could speak to the needs of the river rats, especially those of the women who were sick and dying. Dixie Lou knew what to expect but was concerned about Sunny's ability to deal with these tragic souls. Sunny is such a softie, she thought. So innocent of what a hard life some folks have. Thinks a lot of love— and good tea, of course—can make a remarkable difference in one's life. Hope she can accept that what little we can do tonight may provide fleeting comfort for a few dying women. With a cynical laugh to herself she remembered the nursing she did in Nam and longed to do more.

Chapter Nineteen

A t 8:30, just as the sun was setting, an old broken-down car pulled into the hotel parking lot. As arranged, Dixie Lou and Sunny, now noticeably dirty and tattered, waited at the back delivery entrance. Neither Marcos nor his charges spotted one another right away. Dixie Lou was stooped under the weight of her backpack, gray looking and shaky. She had a little spittle in the corner of her mouth. Under her coat, Jake was incredibly warm and complaining loudly through her clothing. Dixie Lou successfully ignored his noise making.

Sunny leaned heavily on her old walking stick, a bag over her shoulder and Chloe at her side tethered by a piece of old rope. She had soot on her face and kept wringing her hands. The chariot Marcos had obtained was an old black, rusted Honda Civic. The front windshield was badly cracked. The gray upholstery stained and badly torn. Missing a back bumper and sporting a bouncing tail pipe, the Honda looked as if it were snatched from the car cemetery immediately before it was flattened and buried. Dixie Lou, Sunny, Chloe and Jake hurriedly jumped in the backseat. A black man with a heavy accent was in the driver's seat and told them to scoot down and be quiet. Marcos was in the front passenger seat, holding the door shut as its latch was broken.

Under Sunny's overt show of support, she was shaking inside; nervous, worried, concerned about what was to come. Even her chamomile tea over dinner offered little respite from her anxiety. The serenity of the Tea Shop flashed through her mind and she gathered strength from it. Chloe seemed to sense her unease and was more attentive to her than usual. She scrunched down on the floor at Sunny's feet with her head on Sunny's lap, eyes wide open, nose twitching and smelling. Occasionally she panted. The driver put the car in gear, took off, and in no time seemed to stop abruptly.

"Here's far as we go," said the driver, pulling into a darkened corner near the river. "I'll be back here in two hours. If you don't make it, you're on your own." He jumped out, quickly pulled two shopping carts stashed behind a large Dumpster and shoved them toward Dixie Lou and Sunny.

Dixie Lou slid out of the car, excitedly anticipating meeting Juana. She was unaware of the cold and damp night air. She stuffed their purchases into the carts, covered them with newspapers and old dirty blankets Marcos provided, and handed one off to Sunny. "Follow me, Sunny. Keep up now. You too Marcos," Dixie Lou commanded with assurance.

Sunny, hypersensitive to this new environment, cleared her throat as she took in the smell of fish and other debris blowing in from the water. She swallowed with difficulty, choking down fear and bile. She thought she heard a seagull in duet with a fog horn from a phantom barge not too far away. The ground was dark, rocky and slippery, but Sunny followed in Dixie Lou's footsteps as directed, occasionally tripping on Dixie Lou's heels. Unaccustomed to the sound of waves slapping against the pier, Sunny was startled and disoriented at first. Chloe, however, was energized and excited by this new adventure and delighted to once again be a guard dog for her beloved mistress. Jake continued to whine and protest about his secret compartment. He wanted out too. Marcos insisted on leading and headed toward the designated meeting spot along the water. The tension was complex within this group, but their energy and vigilance were concentrated and focused.

"Here we are," Marcos announced softly. He selected a spot with a high bank encased by silent trees. Sunny thought the spot appeared similar to all the others they had bypassed, but Marcos had information about the particular meeting place from his well-connected cousin and knew what to look for. "Yes," he continued. "This is it." Dixie Lou did not question his opinion. "Let's form a little circle, our backs together for warmth, and sit a spell along this shoreline. Put the carts to the side of us," he said.

The small caravan positioned itself and waited for what seemed like a time without end. Finally, silently, Juana appeared along with six other homeless women. In the dark shadows it was hard to tell them apart with only the ambient light from the city streets on the water. There was a great deal of shuffling, coughing, and wheezing coming from these visitors and Dixie Lou reached down in her bag and took out a large Thermos of coffee and a several hot cups. She also took out a first aid pack.

"Hi, I'm Dixie Lou," she said, her accent more Brooklyn than Southern. "This is Sunny, Chloe, and Marcos." Annoyed at being slighted, Jake began squirming violently in Dixie Lou's pocket. Ignored, he began to loudly call out Dixie Lou's name.

"What's that?" questioned one of the women, clearly terrified. "Who said that?"

"No one," Juana immediately replied. "Just hearing things again, Molly. Don't be afraid."

"Naw, I ain't hearing *things*. Those voices sound different from this. I know what I hear and what you people hear. I ain't that crazy! Something is talking from that one's pocket," she said pointing to Dixie Lou. She reached out to grab Dixie Lou's inner pocket when Chloe started to emit a warning growl. Marcos, too, moved closer to Dixie Lou.

"It's okay, stay back," Dixie Lou said to Marcos and Chloe. "It's all right." Turning to the frightened women, Dixie Lou gently spoke. "Molly, member me? From Columbia Avenue. Coupla years ago. And my friend Jake?" She removed Jake from his hidey-hole and held him out to Molly. No one moved. After a few moments, Molly's eyes seemed to clear along with her mind and she broke into a large, and quite attractive smile.

"Jakey, Jakey," she said. "Come here and let me love on you. Talk to me and make me feel good like you used to. Let me give you a little sugar, and squeeze you hard a bit."

Molly's remembrances broke the tension and all the women embraced Dixie Lou simultaneously. In turn, they shook Marcos's hand, and offered Sunny a hug as well. Chloe relaxed and was petted on her handsome head. Dixie Lou passed out paper cups filled with the hot coffee. Sunny was speechless, her fear gone. In its place was deep compassion for these street women.

Sunny watched as everyone's cup was filled and each woman rummaged around in her pockets for packets of powdered milk and real sugar. Most used an inordinate amount of these condiments to enhance their coffee. Dixie Lou reached into her bag and handed Juana a large box of packaged sugar, Sweet and Low, and powdered creamers. Without discussion, Juana simply slipped these gifts into her deep coat pocket and thanked Dixie Lou with a nod and a smile.

Once the group was warmed and comfortable, Dixie Lou began to speak. "Juana," she said, "and friends, usedta be one of you. Molly, you know. You member how we usedta sleep by Pier 82, near the fish warehouse. Warm but smelly as I recall. Anyways, had to move on and landed in Rio Rojo, a place out West. Nice and warm there, good people too. Much easier on my old bones to handle all around. But now I'm back for a visit with my good friends Sunny and Chloe. Marcos is a friend too, a new one. So I need to know how I can help y'all. What's changed and what's needed these days."

While she spoke, Dixie Lou motioned Molly to sit next to her and hold Jake. She began to clean and dress a noticeable wound on Molly's arm. Molly, like a small child, accepted these ministrations and welcomed the tender care and comfort of Dixie Lou. She petted Jake's furry head and shoulders in a repetitive, child-like manner. She seemed to brighten and smile more easily with Dixie Lou's touch.

"That's what we need most," said one very old woman. Her name was Mayme and she had lived on the streets since she was twelve. Her mother threw her out when Mayme began to look like a teenager and her stepfather was suggesting he would like to break her in right. For her own safety, Mayme was sent away with a kiss and heartbreak from her mother. Now in her late seventies, Mayme was the elder stateswoman for this motley crew. Juana was the designated heir and deferred to Mayme's position.

"We need health care. Need a doctor from time to time but mostly need to deal with minor aches, pains, cuts, colds, ya know, the usual. Could use a soft bed nowadays too. And reasonable, predictable warm coffee. Don't worry so much anymore about being mugged or raped. We're pretty much out of that circuit, thank G-d. Just need to be safe, warm, quiet during our time left. Nothing more." The others agreed with gentle nods and soft smiles.

Someone muttered, "Don't need much anymore."

Dixie Lou continued to examine and treat each visitor with little fuss or comment. She was limited by the setting and the light. She knew they all needed a good soak, and then a good exam to be checked out properly.   Again, the triage nurse, administering superficial care for the short term. She had an idea.

"Mayme, Juana, Molly, all of you, listen to me. We're here for a few days and have a lovely hotel room all paid for. Why dontcha come over a few at a time, get cleaned up and let me check you out, have a bite to eat and then go about your business. If you need more care than I can give, I know a doctor at Maimonides Hospital, Dr. Adler, who will treat you. He's good. Let me give him a call and set up something, okay?"

Mayme turned and spoke with her friends privately. Molly was the most hesitant, familiar with doctors and being locked away. She needed her meds, however, in order to remain independent and on the streets where she felt most comfortable. She could move about, act a little crazy on occasion, and get away with it. She could dream about friends like Jakey, even talk about him, without another pill being shoved in her mouth. She was a bright woman like most schizophrenics, and the medication made her feel dull and look dumb. Left alone with a supply of meds, she was able to regulate her illness and function adequately on her own. She agreed to this plan if Juana and Mayme accompanied her to the doctor when necessary. Dixie Lou agreed to go along as well.

Arrangements were made for Marcos to pick up three women at a time at the corner of Columbia Avenue in the morning. He would take them to the rear entrance of the Marriott where Dixie Lou and Sunny would meet them. A long soak in the tub, an exam and treatment by Dixie Lou, a set of new-old clothes and a lounge in a clean bed was on the agenda. After a mid-morning brunch in the room, this routine was repeated with another trio of women. Over the course of two days, Dixie Lou and Sunny cared for seventeen women. Four of them needed to see a doctor and on the third day, Marcos took them with Juana, Mayme and Dixie Lou to a visit with Dr. Adler. After a thorough and thoughtful exam, these women were relieved that there were no major health problems and returned to Columbia Avenue with assurances that they and their friends would always be welcomed at Maimonides Hospital.

Sadly Dixie Lou said goodbye to her street friends. As usual, she wished she could do more. But it was time to let go of this mission and complete their trip. Jake was sad also. Sunny and Chloe felt transformed, reluctant to return to Rio Rojo. Marcos smiled knowingly.

Chapter Twenty

"It's just the altitude," Dixie Lou explained when Sunny and Kate worried about her shortness of breath. The travelers had safely returned home, tired but content. As they recounted their adventures to the boys and Kate, everyone noticed Dixie Lou was breathing with difficulty. She had retold the story but was struggling to talk easily.

"I'm perfectly okay. Not to worry, please'" she implored. "Now, just let us tell you about the theater," she said, poking Sunny to pick up the conversation.

Sunny, eager to share their adventures with their good friends was very worried, as she knew Dixie Lou's breathing problem had resumed on the train ride home. In fact, she'd asked Dixie Lou directly about her health but her concerns were dismissed as needless and the subject was changed. Sunny made a mental note to re-open the topic that evening when they were alone.

"The Theater was lovely, small, very glitzy and ornate. Old but wonderful," said Sunny. "Our seats were center front and we could see the tiniest change in expressions on all the actors. I could hear every word too. The play was great and then Marcos picked us up in the limo right out front just as if we were rich and famous! I've never felt so privileged!" she chuckled. Kate, with a tinge of jealousy having been left out of this adventure, was nonetheless pleased for her old friend.

While Sunny rattled on, Kate recalled her first encounter with Sunny so many years ago. Kate had been with the Busy Bees, the afternoon quilting group at Old Josh when one of the quilters mentioned a young woman in town who was opening the Tea Shop in the Old Town district. Kate was immediately intrigued with the idea of afternoon tea as it suited her fabricated image of sophistication and worldliness. And as a relative newcomer herself, she also wanted to cultivate friendships that would support her self-portrait of gentility and grace. Besides, it was a bit incongruous in a Southwestern town to have a Tea Shop. This incongruity paralleled Kate's sense of not quite fitting in, so she was curious to check it out. When the Busy Bees completed their quilting for the day, Kate hustled out to her Woodie, hopped in and headed toward Old Town. Parking along the wooden boardwalk, she quickly spotted the Tea Shop. It stood alone on a corner of a large piece of property and was decorated with lace curtains, beaded lampshades, and stained glass windows, all rather recycled looking. When she opened the door she smelled peach and lavender.

Serving a few guests was a petite young woman with wild red hair pinned up in a doily-like hair net. She wore a long broomstick skirt and a poet's blouse covered with a lace vest. Her appearance was as unexpected as was the Tea Shop, but somehow it all seemed to fit together. Kate, conservative and cautious by nature, was intrigued with this woman. She wanted to meet her, just didn't know how.

Sunny, noticing the awkward woman at the door, greeted her with "Come in, come in to my shop. Sit down and have some tea. My peach tea is particularly good today." Somewhat pleased but embarrassed with this attention, Kate quickly sat down and hid behind the menu. She took sneak peeks at this lovely, candle-lit shop, noticing the pansy print table cloths, shelves lined with fine china tea pots, fresh flowers on each table and one server, the owner. A hand-painted sign said 'Tealeaf readings by appointment. See the owner.' From the back of the shop behind a hanging quilt Kate thought she heard a baby cooing.

"I'll have the peach tea and cinnamon toast," she ordered matter-of-factly when Sunny re-appeared.

"Tea and toast," Sunny announced and a squawky bird in the corner screeched, "Tea and toast, tea and toast."

Startled, Kate jumped and knocked over her delicate china teacup, shattering it on the wooden floor. "Oh no. Oh no," the bird loudly continued. The baby began crying. Now completely humiliated. Kate wanted to cry too. Sunny was laughing, however, and amiably offered, "Madame Luna did it again, didn't she. Sassy thing. Gets the baby crying. Scares the daylights out of my customers too until they get used to her. Just a sec, have to get the baby," she said, still chuckling with good spirits. "Do hope you will come back often so that you get used to all of us. We're just quite noisy in here."

Kate was completely baffled by Sunny's behavior. Sunny seemed undisturbed about her bone china cup. Indeed, she seemed more concerned about getting the baby and putting Kate at ease. Kate, socially self-conscious tried to live her life according to a set of rules learned through TV shows rather than family life lessons. Goodness knows her family violated every known social circumstance in her growing up years with their loud, unpredictable and rude drinking behavior. She knew her parents would have created a scene in the Tea Shop, for example, blaming the bird and foolish shop owner for disturbing a customer. While Kate knew *not* to do this, she was completely taken aback with Sunny's response to a difficult moment.

"I'm so sorry," Kate stammered. "I, I didn't mean to wake the baby, and I'll gladly pay for your lovely cup. Just, just tell me how much it is or where to get a replacement. I'll go right now and…"

"Don't be silly," replied Sunny, cuddling a tiny baby. "This is simply a great way to become acquainted. I'm Sunny. I own this shop, this is my daughter, Leah, and as you can see, I need help. Please, hold this baby for a second while I clean up your table. Oh, and what's your name?" she added laughing as Kate struggled to hang onto a now squirming Leah.

Stunned, Kate stammered again, "Why, I, I'm Kate. And, I'd be glad to help. Anyway I can." They both laughed then with this awkward beginning as Leah and Madame Luna, mimicking each other, simultaneously giggled as well.

This peculiar introduction began a long-time friendship through which Kate learned that people could be kind without guile, predictable without boredom. Sunny's steady, easygoing nature allowed Kate to develop her stunted personality and begin to believe she was indeed worthwhile and loveable. Kate's setback occurred with her husband, Charles's, disappearance. As she recalled her opportunities for love, she reminded herself that it had been through the constancy of Sunny's friendship that a second chance at love with Jim was made possible.

"Kate," Jim said softly, squeezing her hand at the same time. Used to Kate taking the social lead when the conversation stalled, he didn't quite know what to do. Her quietness was a bit worrisome for him.

"Oh, yes," Kate blurted. "Your trip sounds wonderful. Wishing we could have been there with you two, that's all," she recovered. She smiled with deep affection for Dixie Lou and Sunny but also with gratitude that she had become an integral and valued member of a loving, family-like circle of friends.

Stifling little coughs, Dixie Lou suggested they go home. Sunny agreed, as she was tired herself. "I'll take you home. I'll get the Woodie," Kate declared, leaving little room for discussion.

Chapter Twenty-one

S unny invited Kate in when they arrived at her house. Although Kate was aware of Dixie Lou's exhaustion, she also recognized her best friend's request as a gentle command. Sunny and Dixie Lou quickly curled up in their favorite spots on the couch and overstuffed chair, Chloe at Sunny's feet. Jake was tucked into the cushion of Dixie Lou's chair but seemed to perk up when she sat down. Madame Luna, covered for the night, was quiet but alert. Kate put the teakettle on and filled a plate with peanut butter cookies, a welcome home gift from Sunny's granddaughter delivered on her visit earlier that day. When Kate brought in this simple snack, served her friends, and sat down in her chair, Dixie Lou began speaking. Her voice was stronger than usual and she seemed to have gotten a second wind.

"Kate, Sunny," she began. "Need to say a few things now. Wantcha both to know some things bout me. You've been good friends to me, never askin' a lot. Kinda like Jake. Never askin much about me. Just acceptin' my presence." Turning toward Kate she said, "Must have been a little difficult for you, Kate, I expect. I know you figured I was just crazy, old, and somewhat dodgy."

Kate, ashamed of being so transparent, began to say "I'm so sorry, Dixie Lou. I just…"

"Shush, no need to apologize. Woulda wondered about me myself if I was you. But you each took me into your hearts and I love you for this."

Dixie Lou paused a long moment, sighed, and took a deep breath. She continued, "Been lonely a long time. Heart's been empty quite a while. First, when Mama died and Daddy went inside himself. Was really by myself. Had Jake, thank goodness." For a few moments she seemed to lose herself in thought.

"Growin' up was hard," she continued. "Went to school by myself every day. Daddy left me alone mostly. S'long as I didn't make noise or ask much we were okay together. Had one real girlfriend, Sarah. Spent time at her house with her family much as I could. They observed Shabbot but not like Mama. Much more traditional. Didn't like Jake at the table even. Anyways, Sarah and I talked a lot. Planned our lives. Had a few dreams, hopes. I hoped to meet a kind boy, marry, ya know. Have a real family. A big one. Lots of kids. Pets too. But it didn't happen. I just couldn't find a place for myself, was too much like an orphan. So when I finished school, I left home to nurse the soldiers. Tried nursin' as a civilian after Nam but it just didn't work. All that bureaucracy and paperwork. Little time for the patients even in the Veteran's Hospitals. That was the worst. Young men maimed in mind and body for life. So cynical, angry, despairing. Couldn't take it. Just wanted to help. Felt useless, ya know. Couldn't go back home to Daddy so began wanderin' around this country, lookin' for something to hang on to. When I had money and felt good, volunteered at vet centers, homeless shelters, even soup kitchens. Sometimes ended up using them myself. Nothin' seemed to matter much. Jake kept me going, remindin' me that I could find a place for myself, make somethin' of myself. Make a difference somehow. Course, couldn't really believe him, just an old stuffed teddy bear, right?"

Sunny, somewhat used to Dixie Lou's surprises, was completely stunned with this information. Dixie Lou, the one who helped so many others, who seemed so centered and sure of herself, so respected and loved by many, admitting to feeling unloved, disconnected, alone? Why, it was unthinkable. Kate, too, was astonished with this revelation. She thought she was the only one so insecure and anxious about the need for permanent and deep caring relationships.

"Well," Dixie Lou went on, "now, for the first time that I've found such wonderful friends that I can count on, I have to leave. I..."

Before she could go on, Kate shouted "No," surprising herself as well as the others with her outburst. "I mean, what are you talking about? You're us. Our family. We need you." Further embarrassed about her selfish-sounding position, Kate corrected herself and went on. "I mean, you need us too, don't you? We take care of each other. You can't go off by yourself!"

Sunny, generally patient and polite, jumped in with "No, you can't. Yes, what *are* you talking about, Dixie Lou? Your place is here. With us." Her usual calm, accepting nature was severely threatened with Dixie Lou's declaration, as she knew how much she had grown to depend on her. And she knew Dixie Lou needed them as well.

Sunny had a good sense about people. Having her daughter out of wedlock at such a young age prepared her for adulthood quickly and decisively. She learned early to take care of herself through taking care of others. She rarely acknowledged her emotional needs beyond making others feel good. Over the years Sunny and Leah were accepted into the culture of this small Southwestern town without gossip and criticism. She was well liked and respected as a wise albeit unusual businesswoman and she supported herself and Leah, with Kate's help, for over thirty years through her quaint Tea Shop. Leah had grown into a lovely young woman who married and had two sons and a daughter of her own, the granddaughter Sunny was so close to. Sunny had given her the Tea Shop to manage when she and Kate could no longer keep up the long hours without help. It was this grandchild who knew Sunny better than anyone.

"Dixie Lou," Sunny interrupted. "Don't say such silly things. Kate and I both know you are not well, and we know you need us now. It's time you let someone take care of you for a while."

Kate, surprised at her own need to have this crazy old bag lady remain in her life, went on. "You can't go. We need you. I need you—and even Jake--in my world. You're important to us. To me. I count on you in your own, peculiar manner. Always there, always good, always full of hope. You've taught me so much about people. About how appearances mean nothing. About how what's inside matters," she insisted, her own breath short, anxious. "We'll get you a doctor. Fix you up and you can stay with Sunny forever, right Sunny?"

"Of course" Sunny quickly replied. "With my social security and little nest egg we can manage together. Don't worry about the doctor, either, as our town Doc will treat you without charge. Just don't go, please. *We* need you," Sunny pleaded.

"It's not the money. Not medical care neither," Dixie Lou stated. "I need to do something, special-like. Need to make a difference. Need to make up for all those boys I couldn't make well. Need to make a mark…something important, ya know. Realized it when we visited my old home. Need to help others like my friends on the street. Life's been real good here, but I don't have much time left and there's still much to do."

The depth of this conversation, the evening's activities and the let down of the trip home began to take its toll on Dixie Lou. She began coughing again and her second wind vanished. As if a plug were pulled, she deflated, slumped in her chair a bit and simply stopped talking.

Sunny, sensing Dixie Lou's deep fatigue insisted the three friends call it a night, claiming she herself was exhausted. She and Kate directed Dixie Lou to bed, assuring her they would continue the conversation in the morning. They put Jake alongside on her pillow. Dixie Lou was strangely compliant. So was Jake. For once Chloe slept at the foot of Dixie Lou's bed rather than in her usual place alongside Sunny.

Chapter Twenty-two

D ixie Lou put in a difficult night, coughing and awake for hours. Sunny, too, did not sleep even during the quiet times between coughing spells. She was very worried about her friend. At 4:00 A.M. she got up, made herself some tea, wrapped a serape around her shoulders and with Chloe, went out to the patio to think. The early morning light gently embraced her, and her heart warmed as she considered a plan to address Dixie Lou's welfare. First things first, she would call Kate as soon as reasonable, make a doctor's appointment for Dixie Lou, and then get her up and readied for Kate to pick them up. They would talk after seeing the doctor.

Dixie Lou had not been to a doctor in twenty years or so. She had no medical records, just the confidence that she had managed reasonably well until the past few years when her breathing became labored. In no time, Dr. Johns determined that at best, Dixie Lou had chronic bronchitis which had caused a strain on her heart, or at worst congestive heart failure. In any case, she was to do daily breathing treatments, take a regime of medication, continue to eat and sleep well at Sunny's, and stay in the Southwest. She was not to live outdoors, or travel back East where the weather would be too brutal for her frail condition. While upset with Dixie Lou's diagnoses, Sunny and Kate were thrilled that she was under Doctor's orders to remain with them. They were sure they could improve her condition with their tender loving care.

Dixie Lou knew better. She took the news stoically. Well, she thought, this was to be expected. Too many years bouncing around. Too many times of untreated coughing. Too many cigarettes. Too much exposure to bad air. And too many years on this old body. Better get busy with what I need to do and do it here maybe. Out loud she said, "Okay, let's talk over tea and cinnamon toast. Off to the Tea Shop. Sunny, call and make sure your granddaughter is there."

Sunny's granddaughter prepared the old friends' special table with teacups of assorted design. Sunny loved the yellow rose cup, delicate and fine. Kate, on the other hand, preferred a larger cup with a bigger handle decorated with tulips of various colors. Dixie Lou enjoyed being surprised with the cup du jour. Sunny's granddaughter set a place for herself as well. The milk was warming, and sugar sticks were placed in the center.

As the friends entered the Tea Shop, they were chattering on top of one another. Time and age had conspired to cause Sunny's hearing to decline, and Kate's impatience to increase. "If we have to talk so loud, everyone will hear us," Kate complained.

"So what," replied Sunny. "No one cares about us three old ladies. Figure we're probably talking nonsense anyways. Besides, who's here to hear us?"

Kate retreated into a fond memory for a moment.

When the friends arrived little time was spent in pleasantries with Sunny's granddaughter. Dixie Lou clearly had an agenda and wanted to get to it without delay.

"Well," she said after the tea was poured. "Want to build a home," she declared and paused a moment. "One with lots of windows, a wrap-around porch, and a large kitchen. Don't need anything fancy, just big. Lots of sleeping space too. Maybe we could build it right next to the Tea Shop. Lots of land here. Could even connect it to the Tea Shop so we could travel back 'n forth easy. Could let the boys stay here if they want and some of the gals from the shelter too. Anybody actually that needed to get out of the cold for a bit. Serve a warm breakfast. A little tea and toast, perhaps. Then a light snack a night. Maybe soup, tortillas and beans. Marge could help. Nothin fancy. Just fillin'. Have the money from Daddy's settlement. Need to spend it soon. Thinkin' about this for quite a while now. No good to anyone when I'm dead and gone. Thought I should go back to Columbia Street to help at first but maybe it would work here too. Well?" she finished anxiously looking at her friends' faces.

While Dixie Lou had the vision and resources, she knew she needed her friends' support and help. Would Sunny give up her old adobe home and move to town? Would Kate and Jim want to live with others or remain alone together in their warm cocoon? And Marge, a career waitress, was she ready to slow down and serve light meals in a less hectic environment? What about the boys? Dixie Lou held her breath awaiting their responses.

Sunny's granddaughter was ecstatic. "Absolutely," she said. "What a wonderful idea. I'll help of course. Whatever you need." In this way she could keep a closer eye on her Nana and Nana's friends and at the same time participate in their ever-changing lives more fully. The Tea Shop was doing very well, and she saw herself offering her waitresses as volunteer help whenever needed. Like her grandmother, she embraced adventures with enthusiasm and included others easily within her circle of love.

"Yes," echoed Sunny. "A wonderful idea. We can use furniture from my place to get started. Need space for Chloe and Madame Luna but I take up little room. And I make good tea."

While Dixie Lou was so pleased with Sunny and her granddaughter's response, she knew Kate cast the heaviest vote. Kate's 'what if' nature could dampen their spirits quickly and decisively as the idea, after all, was one for young people, not old women with limited life expectancies. And Kate approached change with such caution, although she had become much more willing to embrace the unknown with Jim in her world. Dixie Lou noticed she was holding her breath and sighed deeply to relax.

"Well," said Kate. "Not one to live in a crowd of strangers usually. But s'long as Jim's willing, so am I. And if the boys hung out from time to time, could be fun. Don't know about those women at the shelter though, or strangers coming in. They were awful nice about the shower I guess. We'd have to leave that up to your judgment, Dixie Lou. Wouldn't mind having a room to quilt. Maybe even start up a junior Busy Bees group for visitors to learn an old craft. Jim would need his own space too, you know. Needs to be away from it all sometimes," she concluded.

The afternoon wore on with the friends making plans and growing more excited about their new adventure. Dixie Lou sat back quietly and listened as the others rattled on crystallizing their dreams for this group home. She was so grateful and relieved that they embraced her idea with such ease and was comforted by their presence. Her throat loosened, her chest opened, and she felt better than she had for a few weeks.

Chapter Twenty-three

After many meetings with the boys, Marge, Jim, Sunny's granddaughter and the elderly principals, plans were designed to build the group's home. Each prospective resident contributed his or her unique ideas and conditions. Jim and Kate needed a small but private suite on the first floor, while Sunny opted for a corner room upstairs overlooking the desert in the distance. Her granddaughter simply wanted the opportunity to sleep over on occasion. Joe and Sam would share a room, they didn't need much, and Bud asked for space in the large living area to host AA meetings on a weekly basis. Marge was thrilled with the task of planning the kitchen and dining areas and welcomed any private space near these facilities. Dixie Lou said little. Her need was simple and constant—to offer respite to any who wanted it. As the major financial contributor, she handed the money over to Sunny's granddaughter for safekeeping and distribution when appropriate. Sunny's job was to plan the garden and landscaping around the porch. Bud quickly offered to be her assistant. Together they happily perused seed catalogues and garden shops to find the best and most hardy perennials available.

It seemed as if the guesthouse, as it was now called, assumed a will of its own. Each step in the building process occurred with speed and ease. The townspeople, initially suspect of the old ladies' dream, began to embrace the concept of a residence for any who needed short-term respite and contributed ideas, supplies, and in some cases, money to complete the project. They saw the guesthouse as a throwback to early frontier living where passersby could stay overnight at a stage stop inn and have a warm, safe place to eat and rest a bit. Church groups and youth clubs joined in to help with the physical labor when possible. The Busy Bees and Women's Club in town held fundraisers to assist with cash donations.

"Pretty funny that that uppity Women's Club wants to help out with our scruffy crew," Kate commented one afternoon as the three women sat in the Tea Shop for a short break from the activities at the guesthouse. "Always thought we were a bit nutty, 'specially after Dixie Lou joined us," she laughed. For the first time in her life, Kate felt respected and authentic. She no longer needed to fake sophistication for approval. In fact, encircled in love from her faithful group of friends, Kate felt blessed.

Jim watched Kate's transformation with quiet joy. He, too, along with the boys, was beginning to risk joining *the world* and trusting in others, a big step for these vets who had become so disillusioned with life. A little magic perhaps.

One evening, after a full day working at the guesthouse, Sunny and Dixie Lou were seated on Sunny's patio, watching the sun set over the mountains. It was especially beautiful as the rocks reflected pinks and purples against a backdrop of gray. As the sun slipped out of sight, the mountains lit up momentarily, as if a flashbulb went off.

Sunny smiled and said, "You know, Dixie Lou, I've been real lucky. Getting pregnant so young, and alone, at first I thought God was real mad at me. Punishing me for loving Leah's father so and not being married, you know. But he wasn't. He gave me a beautiful, healthy baby girl and a chance to make something of our lives. He led me to this town, where people are open and warm, accepting of differences, giving newcomers a chance. These folks supported the Tea Shop much the same way they are now supporting our guesthouse. Good people for sure. And every so often, God reminds us that he is ever present with new and glorious sunsets like tonight."

Cradling Jake on her lap, Dixie Lou was reminded of the evening prayer of thanksgiving her Mama used to recite. While her life had been filled with losses and loneliness, she too had found her safe haven in this southwestern desert town among these good folks. Perhaps she too, could discard her armor of self-sufficiency and dress in the safety of her friends' care and compassion. Jake seemed to sense her thoughts and twitch with excitement. It was time for Dixie Lou to allow herself to be nurtured by others.

One particularly sunny afternoon, Sunny was seated on the porch, rocking with gusto on her new old rocker from the antique store around the corner. She was especially pleased with it as it squeaked with each backward motion and was small and rather squat, perfect for her petite frame. The wood was highly polished in the pattern of the many seats that had occupied it over fifty years of use. At least a dozen other rockers filled the porch, each different yet appealing. Kate enjoyed the one from The Cracker Barrel, a Bentwood, large, sturdy, and quiet. Dixie Lou liked the one with a padded seat and the old afghan over its arm. The boys selected their favorites as well as did Marge and Sunny's granddaughter. There was always an empty one available for a potential guest to use either for a few moments or a few months.

When the guesthouse was completed and occupied by its permanent residents, many people visited and stayed a while. Each left deeply touched with the generosity of this small group of friends who never asked for identifications, home addresses, or social security numbers. No one need qualify for a warm bed, good meals, and a safe haven. The only expectation was that a guest tell Kate, Dixie Lou or Sunny of any medical needs and that they tell others about the guesthouse when they continued on their way.

Dixie Lou's inheritance was diminishing but the townspeople continued to hold fundraisers for the guesthouse. The boys and Marge contributed most of their retirement or disability monies. Occasionally anonymous donations arrived in the mail from Las Vegas with small gifts to assist with the needs of future guests.

Almost like magic, the guesthouse encountered few obstacles and quickly became a source of pride for this small town.

Within a short time, rocking ceased to relax Sunny. She walked into the large living room, sat there a spell and then wandered over to the Tea Shop. She had been feeling anxious, uncommon for her. Oh Sunny had suffered her dark days early in life when she was so young, pregnant, scared, and alone. And although she and the baby were readily embraced by strangers in her new town, Sunny secretly carried the shame of her single parenthood around for years. Like Dixie Lou, she too, cared for others as a way to expiate her own emotional baggage.

Over her long lifetime, Sunny learned to let go of her shame but struggled on occasions with bouts of deep sadness, wishing she could have provided a father for her baby, a husband for herself. Over time, she had had discreet lovers, affairs that lasted for long periods. In fact, Sunny remained friends with several of her former lovers. Rarely though did she feel anxious. Time to visit the tea leaves, she said to herself. She called ahead to ask her granddaughter to prepare the reading room for her.

The reading room was in the back of the shop where Leah's playpen used to be. The old quilt still graced its entrance but was enhanced by a pair of sheer curtains that provided some privacy. A small, round table with two chairs was positioned in the middle of this room upon which Sunny's granddaughter placed a simple white teacup with a wide rim, sturdy handle, and deep bowl. A delicate china teapot that held a steeping bowl of oolong tea was placed in the center of the table. Votive candles and a cedar incense stick were burning on a shelf along the back wall. The little tearoom was like an island of serenity within the bustle of the Tea Shop. Sunny loved visiting her old habitat. She sat down, quieted herself, and began the ritual tea drinking, savoring each sip. When finished, she left a minute amount in the bottom of the cup, held it in her left hand, and twirled it around three times from left to right. Then she turned it over onto her saucer and let the liquid drain away. When emptied, Sunny righted her cup with the handle facing her and slowly peered into it. There were many symbols near the rim of the cup indicating events in the present or near future. Fewer leaves remained at the bottom, indicative of past events. Sunny focused and then concentrated her attention on the assembly of tealeaves.

As usual, Sunny saw the symbol of the dog designating faithful friends and loved ones in her life. The bird was also present, representing good fortune. She smiled at these, affirming their message. She searched for a sign of the bear but was disappointed in its absence. Near the rim she saw a coat suggesting a parting, perhaps the end of a friendship. She also noted the walking stick foretelling the advent of a visitor.

A few leaves on the side looked like a bush. Great, Sunny thought. Fresh opportunities and new friends. When she examined the leaves near the bottom of the cup she interpreted past events—a wedding, good fortune, and a journey—and felt reaffirmed in her belief in the tales of the tea.

The reading took an hour and when finished, Sunny felt renewed. Over the years, reading tealeaves was comforting to Sunny, even when the leaves foretold that the future might hold some difficulties for her. The comfort occurred through the process of self-examination and reflection with the knowledge that good always accompanies bad and sometimes, bad is erased as if by magic with more goodness occurring. Today was no exception. In spite of the foretelling of loss, she returned to the guesthouse feeling relaxed and uplifted.

Chapter Twenty-four:
Today

Not too long after her return from the Tea Shop, Sunny joined Kate in their cheerful kitchen for a few moments of relaxed conversation as only two old friends could have.

"Seems like we've been blessed with our lives here together, don't you agree?" Sunny stated with conviction. "And now we are especially fortunate having Dixie Lou and Jake, and the boys and Marge within earshot for company and friendship. I don't feel so empty anymore, almost full of life as if it is close to finished for me."

"Stop talking like that," commanded Kate, closely observing her old friend for signs of weakness, fatigue, confusion. "You're just fine. A little deaf maybe, but I think you even like it that way since you refuse to get a hearing aid. I don't like it when you talk like this," she concluded.

"Don't worry Kate, I'm okay. Real okay actually for the first time ever," Sunny finished. Changing the subject but retaining her thoughts she suggested, "Let's go out on the porch and sit a while. Go ahead. I'll catch up to you after I put together a pie for dinner."

Relieved Kate agreed and then wandered out to the porch. Dixie Lou had preceded her after lunch and was already sitting, rocking with Jake. They talked for a while when Kate suggested, "How about some tea?"

"Love some," Dixie Lou smiled contentedly and answered. "And maybe some cookies too?"

"I'll get it, and find Sunny. She's been a while and should be finished with that pie by now," Kate offered. "Stay put and we'll be right back." Within ten minutes she returned with a tray of cookies and tea with Sunny in tow. Kate, turning her back to Dixie Lou, set the tray down on a wicker end table and began arranging the teacups and pouring the tea.

Sunny gasped. "Dixie Lou" she said softly. "Oh Dixie Lou, not now, not yet." Dixie Lou had closed her eyes and slipped into death with ease and peace seated in her favorite rocker, wrapped in the afghan with Jake on her lap. Jake, too, was silent. And still.

Within twenty-four hours, a simple memorial service honoring Dixie Lou was held in the large living room of the guesthouse. Sunny and Kate expected this to be a rather small gathering of Dixie Lou's friends but many people from town came to pay their deepest respects as well. Tisha arrived at the last moment, breathless yet reserved and saddened by Dixie Lou's death. She placed a diamond tennis bracelet in a bowl near a picture of Dixie Lou's taken at Kate's wedding.

Those who attended from the shelter brought plastic flowers to place on a table. These women were dressed in an assortment of clothes obviously obtained through a thrift store outlet. Clean, quiet, and somewhat shy they assembled on the sofa in the far corner of the room.

A few newcomers to town who had taken up temporary residence under the bridge also arrived. Many of them wore camy fatigues, vestiges of their earlier lives. Some smelled of cigarettes but none of alcohol. Chairs were hastily obtained from the Tea Shop to accommodate all the guests.

School children came with their parents or teachers with pictures they colored to honor Dixie Lou. Most included Jake in these pictures. They sat on the floor in front of Dixie Lou's photo and placed their handiwork at the foot of the small table.

Members of the Women's Club arrived with food they prepared and set it up in the kitchen shooing Marge away to join Kate and Sunny in the living room. As one looked around the crowded room, the diversity of age, station in life and affluence was remarkable. So many people offered their condolences to Kate and Sunny that they were overwhelmed with the outpouring of love. They had no idea that Dixie Lou had affected so many in her short time as a member of this small town.

Sunny welcomed the guests with a shaky voice and tears flowing down her wrinkled cheeks. "Please," she said looking around, "feel free to say a few words if you will."

Surprisingly, many people had particular and special memories of Dixie Lou that they shared with the others. The enormity of her generosity and kindness were felt by so many of the townspeople. Even children spoke up with special times they recalled when Dixie Lou sat on the porch and listened to their days' happenings, their dreams, hopes, and worries. Her response was always the same—accepting, comforting, encouraging, with Chloe by her feet and Jake in her side. The children felt Jake's assurances as well.

Finally Kate spoke, holding Jake close. "Dixie Lou was a threat to me," she confessed. "My life was finally in order with my best friend, Sunny, and her granddaughter at the center. So predictable. So safe. Then this Dixie Lou came along. A dirty-looking old woman with a stuffed bear she treated as if he could talk. Sunny, of course, took to her like taffy. Even believed that old bear could talk if Dixie Lou said so. I thought my world was disintegrating. Thought it was becoming crazy-like. Felt as if I were back home with my nutty upbringing. I was panicking and just wanted Dixie Lou to go away." She paused, wiped tears from her face, sighed and continued. "Well, she's gone now. And I miss her. I want her back. I need her in my life. She completed Sunny and me. Made me a far better friend. Kept me honest, open even when it was painful. Wouldn't let me get away hiding behind my façade. I became real because of Dixie Lou. Even Jake became real and important. I loved her deeply. She was my sister." With that Kate looked out over the group, smiled slightly, and sat down.

Sunny had little to say. She, too, had been enriched through Dixie Lou. She felt Kate's eloquence said it for both of them. She concluded with a Kaddish prayer she read from Dixie Lou's prayer book and then with the reading of a letter found on a crumpled piece of paper in the pocket of Dixie Lou's favorite oversized sweater.

"To my dearest and most valued family of friends," it began, *"I wish to leave the following:*

To Sunny, the perfect hostess, I leave the guesthouse. Only with Sunny's graciousness, abiding faith in others, sense of adventure and love of the unknown has the guesthouse been possible.

To all the others, I offer permanent residence at the guesthouse with the hope that this home remains open to any and all that need a safe, loving respite for a long time to come.

To Sunny's granddaughter, I give my remaining inheritance for use in the upkeep and maintenance of the Tea Shop and the guesthouse.

To Tisha, adventuress and seeker, I leave my spirit of wandering for the sake of healing.

And to dear Kate, I leave my oldest friend and most faithful companion, Jake, who holds the key to the magic of everyday life."

Epilogue

As months passed, Dixie Lou's absence was felt deeply by the guesthouse residents as well as by the townspeople. She was often mentioned in quiet conversation with respect and love. Jake remained silent, never heard from again. Kate faithfully placed him in Dixie Lou's rocker by day and favorite overstuffed chair by night. Chloe hovered nearby at all times. Madame Luna chattered exclusively with a Brooklyn accent.

One cool morning in late summer a stranger arrived. A tall woman in a tattered raincoat, she stood silhouetted in the morning mist. The rainy season was about to begin, and Sunny sat alone on the porch with Jake alongside. During her usual early morning musings, she had begun talking to Jake as Dixie Lou did, softly though, almost inaudibly, reflecting on Dixie Lou's life, as she knew it. She appreciated the interruption of a new guest. The void of Dixie Lou's death was almost palpable, like a boulder on Sunny's heart.

"Welcome to Jake's Place," Sunny announced to the stranger. "Come, sit a spell. Come on," she insisted. "I need a little company right now and look's like you might be it. Here, hold Jake, would you? I'll go make us some peach tea and we can get acquainted." Jake wiggled.

And the magic begins again.